Where the Wind Blows

RAYMOND HAN

Little Rocket Books

Website: www.raymondhan.net
E-mail: han.raymond@hotmail.com

Little Rocket Books, Singapore
ISBN: 978-981-11-4064-8 (pbk.)

National Library Board, Singapore Cataloguing in Publication Data
Name(s): Han, Raymond, 1958-
Title: Where the wind blows / Raymond Han.
Description: Singapore : Little Rocket Books, 2017.
Identifier(s): OCN 993615997 | ISBN 978-981-11-4064-8 (paperback)
Subject(s): LCSH: Singapore--Fiction. | Dictators--Fiction. | Young adults
    --Fiction.
Classification: DDC S823--dc23

DEDICATION

To my dearest Cindy to whom I owe an
eternal debt of gratitude.

"It is during our darkest moments that we must focus to see the light."

Aristotle

ALSO BY RAYMOND HAN

THE GOLDELL PRISM

SPICE OF LIFE:
SINGAPORE SHORT STORIES

ESSENTIAL GUIDE TO O-LEVEL ENGLISH
COMPOSITION

"And shall come forth; they that have done good, unto the resurrection of life; and they that have done evil, unto the resurrection of damnation."

John 5:29

ACKNOWLEDGMENTS

Thanks to my wife, Cindy, whose unwavering
support has given me the impetus to
complete this my second novel.

VISIT THE AUTHOR'S WEBSITE

Find out more about Raymond Han on his
Website
at www.raymondhan.net

CHAPTER 1

Today was 22 May 2030. It was the last day of the examinations for year-two students at Temasek University, a sprawling campus in Yio Chu Kang. Kuan Hee had just submitted his answer booklet to the invigilator, and was on his way to the lift lobby when he felt a tap on his back. He turned. It was Lina. She was grimacing.

"Have you heard?"

"What about?"

"It's in the news. We have been taken over!"

"You're not making sense, Lina. Calm down and tell me what has happened."

"Here. Take a look at channelsingapore.com." Lina drew out her smartphone and pushed it into Kuan Hee's hand.

"Prime Minister dies. Army takes charge in Singapore," the headline screamed.

"*Alamak*. There goes our future."

"Kuan Hee. Now's not the time to jest around. It's simply horrid. We have come under martial law. You know what that is like? Remember the Philippines? The President there declared martial law back in 2017. What will happen to us here? We will lose our freedom. We will

1

be monitored wherever we go."

"It's not that bad," said a voice from behind them.

"Tim. You are out—finally," said Kuan Hee.

"Well, it was a rather difficult paper. You know I hate Electromagnetic Fields and Waves—I'm going to fail this time. Still all's not lost. I can re-sit the paper."

"Why bother taking up EEE?"

"Nano-electronic devices. Nanotechnology—that's where the future is. That's where I'm heading," quipped Tim, spreading out both arms in front of him and looking upwards as if he was contemplating some great idea.

"For goodness's sake, stop it," stammered Lina. "The whole world's coming to an end, and here you are— carving out your sweet dreams in the air."

"Don't be s-e-r-i-o-u-s. It's the end of the exams. Time to party!"

"Look, Tim. Lina's right. Looks like we may not have jobs waiting for us when we graduate."

"Ha? What are you guys mumbling about? It's not that bad right?"

"Here! Take a look at today's headlines. Mr Chiam Toon Boon has suddenly died. And a new guy is in charge—Colonel Tee Bak Chai. Yeah, that's his name, alright."

"Gosh. Who's this chap? Never heard of him."

"We soon will hear more—and lots more, I reckon."

"It says here he's commander of the elite FF brigade. He'll be making an announcement on TV at 6:00 p.m."

"Rare surname—Tee. Like our Ah Tee."

"You mean Jordan Tee, the tall footballer."

It was getting noisy in the lift lobby. The rest of their course mates were pouring into the lobby. The resultant chatter of voices was deafening. Everyone was trying hard to be heard. Obviously, news of the takeover had spread. Everyone looked glum. Two hours ago, all were in high spirits as it was their last paper for the semester. Now, it seemed someone had dropped a huge bomb into their midst.

"Kuan Hee. Kuan Hee," said a voice from somewhere in the crowd. Navin appeared.

"Kuan Hee. You are our student leader. Tell us what we should do."

"Let's wait for Jordan. He's the senior here. But I don't see him anywhere."

"You can't miss him. He's always wearing his NY baseball cap."

"Speak of the devil—there he is. Down there in the car park. He's being fetched somewhere by some guys in tucked-out shirts."

"Looks like he's being thrown into the car."

"*Aiyah.* You really like to exaggerate things, Tim. He's merely being shown the way into the car—you are very *kaypoh*, you know."

"Hey. Look over there."

"What?"

"To the right—here come some three-tonners."

The army trucks stopped in the car park and a score of soldiers jumped off one of them. These soldiers were armed with rifles. One shouted some commands and they filed up the car park to the main building.

"They are NSmen," said Tim.

"They must have been enlisted after we ORD," said Kuan Hee.

"What's going to happen next?" asked Lina.

"I wish I knew—let's get out of here before these guys seal off the place," said Kuan Hee.

The threesome made their way to the MRT station, a stone's throw away. Even a trained eye could make out nothing out of the ordinary on the road. There were no soldiers along the way. At the station, the crowd was thicker than usual. But, most were students from the nearby polytechnic. As Kuan Hee, Lina and Tim lived in Hougang, they had each other for company till the train arrived at Hougang MRT Station.

Nobody was home at 79 Jalan Naung, a semi-detached house among a clutch of terrace houses. Kuan Hee had lived here all twenty-three years of his life. The only child of a scientist and student care teacher, he had no lack of attention at home. However, he was pretty much alone most of the time. And he had grown accustomed to growing up sans sibling fights and tussles. The blaring of an Internet screen on the wall in the bedroom interrupted his thoughts.

> We bring you the six o'clock news. Prime Minister Chiam Toon Boon passed away at 6:45 a.m. today. The government is concerned that certain elements may take advantage of the situation to launch a terrorist attack on the country. It has appointed Colonel Tee Bak Chai, Commander of the FF Brigade to take charge of the country. To facilitate detection of terrorist elements, there will be an island-wide curfew from 9:00 p.m. till 9:00 a.m. tomorrow. All residents are to remain indoors during the curfew period. Regular programming will now resume.

It was a short news segment that attempted to make normal of the situation in the country. Colonel Tee did not appear on the news programme. Everyone said—trust the Prime Minister. The Prime Minister said—trust my men. This then started the journey down the road to perdition. And it all began with trust.

Kuan Hee's mother poked her face in the doorway.

"Kuan Hee. I've bought fried rice for you," she said. "Your father won't be home tonight. He's busy at work— And, we need to talk, dear." Having said her piece, she turned back into the corridor.

"You're not making dinner tonight? Mum?—Mum?"

He did not get an answer. Perhaps, she had not heard him.

Downstairs in the dining area, as they were eating, Bertha broached the matter of the army takeover of the country.

"Kuan Hee, we must remain calm," said his mother, moving a hand to clasp his hand. Her voice was almost inaudible. There was a slight quiver in it as she continued.

"Kuan Hee—your father—your father he—the army has taken control of the defence agency where he works. He can't leave the complex for the next few days."

"Huh?"

"It seems—I mean this group that has taken control has put restrictions on entering and leaving all military installations—You know your father is doing secretive work for the defence ministry. He—he may not be coming back for a while."

"Has he called back? Have you talked to him? Did he say anything?"

"He called me at the workplace. He couldn't use his smartphone. They have banned all phones—for the time being. I can't reach him now. All calls to the agency are screened by an operator. She keeps saying he is unavailable. I just don't know what to do."

"What did Dad say?"

"We didn't get to talk long. He hinted there was someone beside him. He—he just said he was fine. He wants us to look after each other."

"Sure. No problem, Mum. Can we go visit him?"

"The curfew will come into effect in less than two hours. We have to hurry. I—I'm not sure we will get to see him—But we need to try—I'm worried sick."

"Mum—Mum, we'll be alright."

"Looks like—I think our freedom has been curtailed. Someone has grabbed power—and the government is in disarray."

Kuan Hee had no way to understand the full impact of the situation. The Singapore he lived in was like a dream country in others' eyes. All over the world, people had been flocking here to make a living, to set up home, or send their children for an education. Singapore was, in their eyes, the ideal place to be in. There was hardly any corruption. No one intentionally stopped anyone for a bribe. It was safe for women and girls to wander in the streets in the wee hours of the morning. And everything worked like clockwork—almost everything, except for the MRT system, whose frequent breakdowns continued to put a dent on people's expectations of the public transport system. Still, the MRT system was loads better than those in the neighbouring countries.

Indeed, Singapore was a haven for foreigners. Locals, however, took for granted its efficiency and cleanliness. They had been lulled into complacency by decades of pampering by the government which saw to their every need—so much so that they couldn't care less what happened in bureaucracy or who was in charge of what. It wasn't important. There was ample food on the table. Most owned their own homes, albeit HDB type—but still much bigger than the flats in Hong Kong. And life was easy and convenient. That was what counted, in their eyes anyway. The younger set—those born after 1960—had not been privy to the suffering of their parents and grandparents most of whom have since left this earth.

What a change these locals would go through in the months and years ahead—nobody knew, but anyone could hazard a guess from looking at overseas examples of military-run countries. There was no need to look far—some neighbouring countries held lessons for them.

For Kuan Hee, who had been living in the lap of luxury by foreigners' comparison, it was the same attitude. The mandatory national service he had struggled through a year ago held no meaningful lesson for him. He merely took it as a rite of passage that every Singaporean man had to pass—and then forget. That's it. Period. He had yet to be called up for reservist duties so there was no urgent reminder to him that the security of the country was something no Singaporean should take for granted. Blame this lackadaisical attitude of young Singaporeans on the previous government. On the one hand, it did a remarkable job making the island state livable and enjoyable for its people. On the other, this bred ignorance and almost total abhorrence of participation in national issues. Yes—blame it on the government. It created a good life for its people, but neglected to guard its own kitchen. It forgot that man was greedy by nature—that man was hungry for power—that with power came money and lust. Yes, money, lust and power—these three things reared their ugly heads every now and then;—one or more of them had caused tumultuous changes all through man's history.

All said, no one could actually predict what secrets a face held. And Colonel Tee's was one that held many secrets. To his superiors, he was ever ready at their side, pandering to their needs. Who could resist fawning attention? He was the perfect example of a Yes man—except, he was merely acting. Ever the opportunist, he saw a chance to take power. He had soldiers. He moved around in high government. He had access to many government departments. He was trustable. The Prime Minister was pleased with his performance. And, this moment in time, he saw the right situation—The Prime Minister was alone with him in the study at Dalvey Estate. Both had been spending the wee hours of the morning poring through documents on a terrorist group that had been attacking a littoral country. According to intelligence, Singapore was soon to be the next target. The PM's minders—bodyguards by another name—were downstairs taking an early breakfast. There were no CCTV cameras in this room where the PM spent most of his time marrying personal and official matters.

It was indeed the perfect time—just before dawn. He came up behind the PM who was typing something on the screen. One jab on the neck was all it took to down the man. As the PM lay slumped in his chair, he gave some instructions over his wrist-watch phone. In minutes, the PM's minders would be coming up the stairs. He had to work fast to neutralize the communications network in the house. There was no one in the sitting room upstairs. The computer servers were in a pantry-like room next to it. He scanned a card on the screen next to the room. Once inside, he pulled out the cables behind the servers. That would shut down all communications with the outside world. He reached behind a tall cabinet and his fingers touched something cold. *Good. Nobody has noticed it*, he thought. He retrieved the gun, pulled out the magazine and snapped it back in.

Next, he had to take care of the minders—two in the pantry below, two in the servants' quarters next to the kitchen, and another two at the main gate. The house sat in the middle of a big garden—by Singapore standards—on top of a slope. It would be difficult taking out the guards from the road. The PM's wife was in the second bedroom on the other side of the sitting room. He needn't worry about her—she was a late riser. The couple had no children.

Once downstairs, he readied the Glock 19—one of the good things about a Glock was that it didn't need to be cocked, so there was no sound that would warn others—and leaned against the wall outside the pantry. He had seconds to take out these two minders—the report of the gun would send the last two minders scurrying here and raising the alarm. The next shift of minders would be here at 7:00 a.m. That's thirty minutes from now.

Two shots were all it took to take down the two minders. And they were accurate—between the eyes. Yes, he had not lost his touch, despite being out of practice for years. Once a ranger—always a ranger. He had spent his prime years as a ranger in the Special Operations Forces.

He took aim at the kitchen door—the two minders

outside would be coming through that door in seconds. He fired another two shots as the door opened, and the minders dropped onto the floor. They would have alerted the Operations Centre in Pearl's Hill. But, he didn't have to worry—the security minders had no access to the Command Room at the Ministry of Defence. They could only activate the police patrols. These were of no worry to him. The PM's wife was the least worry—She was a sound sleeper.

He stepped over their bodies and moved towards the main gate. He took down the last two minders who were running towards him. Then he whispered into his wrist-watch phone. His men were waiting at a fork in the road.

Two vans rolled up the driveway into the compound. Out jumped several men—all in tucked-out shirts. They saluted him and went about their tasks. It seemed they had been briefed exactly what they had to do. The PM's wife was awoken and dragged, together with a maid, into a servant's room. Then a huge truck lumbered into the compound. Out stepped a stout man who offered him a salute too. Colonel Tee got into the truck with the man. Inside, there were computer screens on the wall panels. There was a long counter top with telephones and foldable computers. Three other men were at the counter, typing furiously at the screens in front of them.

"Have you neutralized the Command Centre?"

"Yes Sir. Our men are in the Command Centre as of now. We are now communicating with them. Things are working as planned."

"How about the Chiefs of Army, Navy and Air Force?"

"They are in good hands, sir."

"Good. And the Deputy PM, and the Defence and Homeland Security Ministers?"

"Our men have them in custody."

"The police? We have to deal with them too."

"The police commissioner is in custody. And we should be taking over their Operations Centre in twenty minutes."

"The TV station—"

"We have control of the TV and radio stations."

"The Singapore Tribune?"

"Han is there talking to the editors of the newspapers in the News Holding Group now."

"And the border checkpoints?"

"All under control, sir."

"I want the guys at the border checkpoints to be alert. No government official must slip out of the country."

"Yes sir. What about the Minister for Foreign Affairs? He's still in China."

"No need to bother about him. The power rests with the PM. And he's—taking a long rest from politics—and this world."

"Send the order—all men in our foreign stations to be confined to barracks until further notice."

"Yes sir."

"And I want the commanders to fly back for a meeting this afternoon."

"Yes sir."

"Also, confine the Commando Unit to quarters. Place a heavy guard there—use our rangers."

"Yes sir."

"Who's in Mandai?"

"Captain Damien Tan, sir. He's now getting the tanks fuelled and ready to move out."

"Good. We can't afford to be slipshod. Our lives are at stake. We can't eliminate all obstacles in one fell swoop. But, we can try our best."

"I agree with you, sir."

"Warren,"

"Sir?"

"Use the tanks sparingly. I don't want to damage the roads. It's going to be expensive repairing them. Use more armored personnel carriers."

"Yes sir."

"It's going to be a long day."

"Yes, certainly so, sir."

"My wife? Have you got people there too?"

"We were already there just before you left for Dalvey Estate. And your son, sir, we are picking him up after school."

"Thank you. Good job, Warren."

"No worries, sir."

"The PM's guards will be here any time now with reinforcements—"

"Two armored personnel carriers are now outside—on the road. We have a squad of rangers hidden in the surrounding area. No one can get through them."

"Good. Dawn is breaking. Singapore is waking to a brand new government. I'll lead our people to greater heights."

"Of course, sir. I'm sure you will, sir."

"Warren, I need to freshen up. I need to get ready."

"The American Embassy, sir?"

"Yes. We have got to appease the American Ambassador. We must not forget—they are Goliath; we are David."

"But, the American Naval Base has long gone from Sembawang, sir."

"Yes—but they are still quite near—in Australia. Got to calm them down."

"Yes sir."

"Do we have people outside the place?"

"No, sir. I'll see to it sir."

"Assign more people there. Get Steven over there. He'll know what to do. We need to stop people going in to seek asylum."

"Yes, of course, sir."

"We have now gotten control of the most modern armed forces in SE-Asia—fighter aircraft, submarines, destroyers, tanks, and our eye in the sky, the SG17. Our neighbours won't risk offending us. It's only the

Americans and Chinese whom we need to manage carefully."

"Sir, won't the Foreign Minister give trouble?"

"Not to worry. Chiam didn't treat the Chinese well. As long as we pander to them, we'll be okay. Gosh. I plain forgot. I'll have to visit the Chinese Ambassador too, afterwards."

"Yes, sir."

"Shall I dispatch some people there too?"

"No need. Chiam's people won't go there. They know the Chinese won't welcome them—not after what Chiam did to them in 2027."

"You mean, when he commented that the Hong Kong people should be given a choice in universal suffrage?"

"Yes. And of all times, he chose to do so during the thirtieth anniversary of the former colony's handover to China. What a laugh."

"Certainly so, sir."

"Narayanan won't be able to get the Chinese to help him. Remember yesterday's news? They even gave him a cold shoulder. Fancy him—giving them expertise and guidance on developing their cities, and instead of thanks, receiving a lukewarm response during the city-handover ceremony. Hahaha."

"And the Internet, sir. Don't you want to reconsider your decision?"

"No. Not yet anyway. We need to keep business going. The last thing I need is to stir up animosity in the business community. Don't pull the plug on Internet access—yet."

"I understand. Sir, one last thing."

"Yes?"

"The bodies in the house. Should we…"

"Incinerate them at Senoko."

"Aye, aye, sir."

Shots rang out in the distance. More shots followed. Then, came the rumbling of heavy vehicles—and rapid machine gun fire. There was a succession of rapid gun fire.

Then, silence fell again.

CHAPTER 2

It was almost 8:00 p.m. Kuan Hee drove furiously through the long meandering road. His mother was next to him. There was a long silence. Neither spoke a word; but loads were spoken; albeit in their minds. They didn't need to speak to tell each other things. Their heavy hearts showed the way into each other's intimate spaces. Both were intent on seeing their beloved one.

It was 8:26 p.m. when they arrived outside the main gate of the huge Defence Agency complex in Changi East. Two soldiers were at the checkpoint; one approached the car. They were not allowed to enter the complex. Neither were they allowed to see the elder Wang. They couldn't speak to him through an intercom. Even their request to leave a note for him was turned down. Dejected, they left for home. It was a solemn mood in the car. Both said nary a word. As Kuan Hee drove on, the car's headlights pushed back the darkness of the night in front of him. But no sooner, the darkness swallowed what's left of the light behind the car. It was the same with their hearts.

At Jalan Eunos, a thoroughfare, bright spotlights flooded a section of the road, dazzling Kuan Hee's eyes. It was a roadblock. There were soldiers on both sides of the road. An armored personnel carrier was parked on the road shoulder. Sitting atop the carrier, with both hands on a machine gun, was a soldier. A soldier on the ground shone a light into the car, waving his arm to signal Kuan Hee to stop the car. He obliged immediately. He hadn't realized it—but the curfew was in effect. These soldiers were conscripts, barely nineteen years old. After giving a verbal warning, the soldier waved him on. There were hardly any vehicles on the road. Most people obeyed the curfew order; locals had been conditioned through the years to be reticent—they needed no prodding to toe the line. They were unlike Hongkongers who would challenge any order they deemed unfair. Perhaps, that was why Hong Kong thrived against the odds. Their people were resilient. The locals here were lethargic—to use a euphemism, they were untested; they had yet to find good reasons to protest—life was just too good to them, thanks to the government.

It had been a long day. Kuan Hee was dead tired. He plunked himself on the bed and fell into dreamland. His mother was awake throughout the night. Dad and Mum were very close. She couldn't sleep knowing he wasn't safe.

Army seizes power, declares curfew

This was what greeted Kuan Hee as he sat down for breakfast. He scanned the front page of the The Singapore Tribune, then flipped the front few pages, and digested the content. Prime Minister Chiam had died of a heart attack; the government ministers were said to be incompetent and corrupt. Hence, they were being detained. The President was under house arrest pending investigation of his role in colluding with corrupt ministers. Public gatherings were banned.

"Kuan Hee, it's just a pack of nonsense."

"For sure, Mum."

"Our government ministers have always been whiter

than white. I hope they are alright. I hope their families are safe."

"Mum, Dad's coming back soon. Don't worry."

"Yes, I hope so. I've always thought his job with the Defence Agency involved some risk. But, never in my imagination did I expect it to turn out this way."

"I'm not going to class today, Mum. I'll keep you company."

"Kuan Hee, I thought we should try to see your father—afterwards."

"That's my thought, exactly, Mum."

WHATSAPP:
"Meet at usual place at 11:00 a.m.?" texted Lina.
"K," texted Kuan Hee.
"Sure," texted Tim.

It was business as usual at the shops in Hougang Mall; people were streaming in. McDonald's restaurant was humming with activity, though it was not lunch time yet. People were chattering away; they were trying to make sense of the happenings the day before. Like them, Kuan Hee and company, huddling in one corner, tried to dissect the reports on news Websites. Tim unfolded the iPad and bent the screen so everyone could read the print on the screen.

"What does the New York Daily say?" asked Lina.

"Just a short paragraph under the heading 'Army takes power in Singapore'," said Kuan Hee.

"See this? The China Telegraph says: Singapore wakes up to a coup," said Tim.

"All have neutral comments. None has taken a stand in this," said Kuan Hee.

"They are simply adopting a wait-and-see attitude," said Tim.

"What about Malaysia?" asked Lina.

"Let's see: PM Wahab urges calm in Singapore," said Tim.

"Our neighbours appear to be neutral too," said Kuan Hee.

"Look. The Indonesians are asking for restraint," said Tim..

"The Internet forums are abuzz with adverse comments on the takeover. I can't see a single in support of it," said Kuan Hee.

"Any bigwigs commented?" asked Lina.

"Nope," said Tim.

"Someone has set up an online petition 'STEP DOWN COLONEL TEE'," said Kuan Hee. "And it's garnered 37,118 votes as of now."

"Here's another Website. The contributors are calling for the Police to step in and stop Colonel Tee," said Tim. "Hahaha. That's rather lame."

"STEP DOWN COLONEL TEE has hit 41,022 votes," said Kuan Hee.

"That's amazing," quipped Lina. "See this link? Click on it, Tim."

"OK. It's a call to stage a mass protest at Hong Lim Park," said Tim.

"Yes. Says here to meet at 9:00 a.m. 24 May 2030— That's tomorrow," said Lina.

"Strange," said Tim.

"What?" said Kuan Hee and Lina in unison.

"We are browsing the Internet now, right?" said Tim.

"So?" said Lina.

"So—that means the coup perpetrators have not shut down the Internet," said Tim.

"Oh yeah *hor*," said Lina.

"Maybe—maybe, they plain forgot," volunteered Kuan Hee.

"Not so, I think," said Tim. "It must be a tactical move. Sly old man."

"Please make sense of your words," pleaded Lina.

"I know what you mean, Tim," said Kuan Hee. "The old chap most probably knows that he can't shut down the Internet without shutting down communication," said Kuan Hee.

"*Hah*?" said Lina.

"Singapore needs to keep businesses running. Businesses need communication networks for their supply chains, etc.," said Kuan Hee.

"And if you shut down the Internet, that means Singapore goes out of business," said Tim. "Which means—the old man has his hands tied."

"Hurray for Singapore," said Lina.

"Hold your horses, Lina," said Tim. "Don't get so excited, for goodness's sake."

"Why?" asked Lina.

"Because—because," said Tim. "Here, Kuan Hee, you tell her."

"I really don't know," said Kuan Hee. "Sooner or later, he's going to do something about the Internet. What with all these negative comments and calls for protests."

"Yeah. It's just a matter of time, Lina," said Tim.

"Yeah. And then we'll become another North Korea," said Kuan Hee.

"Oh, really?" said Lina.

"Yeah, really, Lina," said Kuan Hee.

"Kuan Hee, I…I think that's stretching the truth a little," said Tim.

"But—it's a possibility," quipped Kuan Hee.

"Lina, just being curious," said Tim. "But—why do you like being with us?"

"Because you are both very clever," blurted Lina.

"And you are stupid?" said Tim.

"*Aw*. You are being horrid," said Lina. "Kuan Hee."

"Knock it off, Tim—Knock it off," said Kuan Hee. "She's going to cry—she's really going to cry."

"Sorry, Lina," said Tim. "Just jiving, Lina."

"You better not do it again," said Lina. Her eyes were

tearing. She was sniffling. "Or else—I'll complain to my mother about you."

"Guys, guys. Let's get serious," said Kuan Hee. "Now's not the time to fool around."

"So, guys—are we or are we not joining the protest?" asked Tim.

"Let's go for it," all three said in unison.

"I've got to go now. Got to visit my Dad, you know," said Kuan Hee.

"Can I tag along?" asked Lina.

"Yeah, can we?" said Tim.

"Sure—I don't think my mother would mind," said Kuan Hee. "In fact, I think she'll welcome the company."

"Let's make a move," said Tim.

The wind blew in noisy gusts across them, dishevelling their hair as they walked towards Jalan Naung. Hougang, whose name is *Hokkien* for 'back of the river', was known for strong winds blowing across this sleepy town. But, for the country, strong winds were heralding change.

The drive to Changi East was interrupted by several stops—there were checkpoints along the way on the main roads of the island, with conscripted soldiers manning them. When they reached the start of Changi Road, they had to turn back—the whole stretch of road leading to Changi East was now off-limits to everyone, except military personnel.

It was the second trip in vain for the Wangs, and despondency fed their growing unease.

WHATSAPP:

"Location of protest has changed," texted Lina.

"Why?" texted Kuan Hee.

"Because army has sealed off Speakers' Corner," texted Lina.

"Where now?" texted Kuan Hee.

"Orchard Road junction—where it meets Scotts Road," texted Lina.

"K," texted Kuan Hee.

"Tim?" texted Kuan Hee again.

"Think he's bathing or something. No response; will try again," texted Lina.

"OK," texted Kuan Hee.

"Meet you at MRT Station @10:00 a.m.," texted Lina.

"K," texted Kuan Hee.

When the threesome arrived at Orchard MRT Station, it was already flowing with people. They elbowed their way up the stairs onto the pavement outside Wisma Atria. People were everywhere—the crowd spilled over onto the walkway outside. There had to be at least ten thousand of them on this part of Orchard Road—the young, middle-aged and elderly. It was noisy with portable loudspeakers blaring away in the street. Some twenty-somethings were using loud-hailers, while some others were holding up cloth banners scribbled with slogans. The trio could not hear themselves above the cacophony of sounds. There were policemen in the street, on the sidewalks—everywhere, but they did nothing to stop the protesters who were out in full force today.

Some protesters had formed a train, and were snaking around the junction, then down towards Lucky Plaza. This group wore yellow headbands fashioned out of cloth. The atmosphere was chaotic. But, amidst disorder, there was some semblance of order. Most protesters had their sights trained on a figure near the bus-stop outside Tang Plaza. He was surrounded by some twenty-somethings bearing rolled-up banners and placards. From where the three were standing, on top of the escalator outside Wisma Atria, they could see as far as the Paragon building. More people were pouring into the streets from the MRT station. There was just no end to the human traffic. Indeed, it was a sea of people.

At last, the figure near the bus-stop spoke. His voice thundered through the loudspeakers. He spoke against the army takeover in the country. He asked the audience to stand up for their rights. He urged all present to join him in putting down the coup.

Suddenly, there was the rumbling of heavy vehicles in the distance. Then, the tops of armored personnel carriers could be seen emerging from Scotts Road, at the junction. The vehicles loomed into view. There were soldiers manning machine guns atop the vehicles. Soldiers were amassing near these vehicles. There were at least six armored personnel carriers and scores upon scores of soldiers bearing rifles. Some shouts were heard coming from the vehicles. Some soldiers were holding video cameras; they were filming the protesters and everyone else. The protesters were getting restless. Some leaders were cajoling them to march towards the armored personnel carriers. The crowd was getting agitated.

A soldier, probably a senior army officer—he was wearing a peaked cap whilst the others were in helmets—screamed through a loud-hailer. His voice echoed through the street. He was telling everyone to disperse. But, nobody was paying heed to him. They were chanting slogans, egged on by the protest leaders. The chanting rose in intensity. The protesters locked their arms with one another. Row after row of protesters moved slowly towards the armored personnel carriers. The trio were undecided. Should they join those in the street. Or should they remain perched on the raised walkway. They didn't have a choice. Waves of people behind them pushed them, step by step, inch by inch, down the stairs, into the street below. There was hardly any room to move. But there was no way they could fall—the whole street was full of people, packed like sardines in a humongous can.

Though tired and wary, the protesters refused to bulge

from the junction. The army did not use water cannons on them. Probably it had failed to convince the police, who had such equipment, to bring them along. Even the policemen seen here and there did nothing beyond keeping a watch on the crowd. Perhaps, they were under orders to remain neutral.

Then, a loud whistle rang out across the road. A long line of soldiers, all standing abreast of one another, raised their rifles and pointed them skywards. At a second whistle, they fired a volley of shots. Were these live rounds? No one in the crowd knew. But, it worked wonders. The crowd stepped away from the soldiers. They were still in locked arms, but it was clear—all were frightened. Everyone wanted to protest, but when it came to the crunch, their life was more important than the idea of freedom—Freedom from tyranny was a worthwhile pursuit—but not the cost of losing their lives. Only the group of twenty-somethings—the ones with their leader near the bus-stop were steadfast in confronting the armed soldiers. Were they mad? Was freedom from control of the soldiers that important? After all, life was still the same—almost. The MRT trains were running; people held on to their jobs; and there was ample food for everyone.

Soldiers moved towards the twenty-something group. They forcefully moved these protesters away from the others. It was then that someone fired a shot into the crowd—or it seemed so. Pandemonium set in. People ran helter-skelter in all directions. There was chaos in the street. Everyone was running for cover, oblivious to the aim of the protest. Some people were falling; some others were stepping onto them. Nobody cared. Nobody took heed.

"Lina—Lina," shouted Kuan Hee. "Run!—follow me."

"Here. This way, quickly," said Tim.

"I'm trying to run as fast as I can," said Lina.

"Oops! I just stepped on something—somebody," said Lina.

"Here, Lina, let me hold your hand," said Kuan Hee.

"Aaargh!" cried Lina. "My arm—it's painful."

"See the opening in front, Tim?" said Kuan Hee.

"Yeah," said Tim.

"Let's head that way," said Kuan Hee.

"Oh no." The soldiers are in front—turn back, Tim," screamed Kuan Hee.

"I can't—there're too many people here," cried Tim.

"It's too late. They have got me, Kuan Hee," said Tim. "Run. Run!"

"Lina, keep up with me," said Kuan Hee.

"I'm trying—I'm trying," said Lina.

"Gosh. We've run into a dead end," said Kuan Hee.

"Alamak!" said Lina.

"Here. Let me lift you up," said Kuan Hee. "Step onto my shoulder. Grab the pole up there."

"What about you, Kuan Hee?" Said Lina.

"Stop talking and get moving," said Kuan Hee. "On the count of three. one—two—three—up!"

"Now run, Lina," said Kuan Hee.

"I can't—I can't leave you," said Lina.

"Go! Don't look behind, Lina," said Kuan Hee. "Aargh!"

Both Kuan Hee and Tim had been captured, but Lina managed to get away. She cried all the way to the back of Paterson Road. No, the world wasn't coming to an end. It was only Lina's world in tatters. She wanted to go back for Kuan Hee. Alas, she couldn't. It was just too late. Kuan Hee was right; she had to go home now. She was of no help to them.

Kuan Hee was ushered into a large bus parked along Scotts Road. There was a score of them, lined up against the side of the road. He did not see Tim. There were too many faces around him; he did not recognise any of them. The soldiers were fresh-faced recruits—NSmen. It seemed that they had just finished basic military training. Or they could still be undergoing BMT. The buses were packed with protesters. All wore anxious expressions. It seemed they were unaccustomed to being in custody. It wasn't local culture; locals did not get hauled into buses. They crammed into buses on their way to work or school—on their own free will, that is.

The buses started their journey to an unknown destination. There were three armed soldiers to a bus. It was quiet inside the buses; everyone was in deep thought—worried about themselves, asking themselves what trouble they had gotten themselves into. Kuan Hee was different. He was worried about Tim and Lina. *Has Lina gotten home safely?* he wondered.

Half an hour into the journey, Kuan Hee realized the buses were heading to SAFTI. They were in the far end of Jurong. SAFTI was only minutes away. It was a familiar route to Kuan Hee, for he had spent the first nine months of his national service in SAFTI. It was a sprawling military installation, probably half the size of Toa Payoh Estate. But there were no detention facilities in it, he was sure. It wasn't built to house detainees; it was training grounds for recruits and officer cadets. He knew the place like the back of his hand; he could almost find his way around it blindfolded.

The buses turned into the main gate at SAFTI. Then, they moved ahead, made a left turn, and rumbled towards the Non-Commissioned Officers' training block. Some came to a stop in the parade square of the Mike Company, while others continued along the road towards Kilo Company. In the compound of Mike Company, a soldier shouted at those in the buses to alight. Everyone gathered in the middle of the parade square. And the buses left after unloading their human cargo.

There were soldiers seated at some GS tables in front of the square. The detainees were ordered to line up in single file behind each table. They were being processed for detention. Their identity cards were retained, kept in a locked metal box. All their personal belongings—smartphones, wallets, keys, etc.—were taken away from them and placed in plastic bags, with their names written on them. Then, they were herded into the different dormitories in the premises. There were twenty bunks in the dormitory which held Kuan Hee. But, there were thirty of them. *Some will have to sleep on the floor*, he thought. The layout of the place was still the same. Kuan Hee remembered the stand-by-beds he had to endure in this place. He recalled being made to do push-ups for not keeping his belongings tidy. And, yes, that bed was where some guy had poured instant glue on his hair while he was sleeping. He had complained to his trainers but they had dismissed it as a harmless prank. Till today, he did not know who had carried out the prank on him. He didn't think he was unpopular then; but, he could have offended a fellow recruit.

Kuan Hee looked out of a window. There were some soldiers smoking in the corridor opposite. Their rifles were resting against the wooden wall of a room. *Typical recruit mentality*, Kuan Hee thought to himself. He was like them till he was reprimanded by an *Enche*. He remembered the punishment—two cold nights doing guard duty at Serimbun, a deserted military training installation by a river. A jeep unloaded him there and left only to return the next morning. The place was eerily quiet and he had nobody for company.

A gunshot rang out in the distance, snapping Kuan Hee out of his thoughts. Fellow detainees in the room leaned against the windows, pressing their faces against them, eager to find out what was happening, but, at the same time, fearful of what lay in store for them.

"Did they shoot somebody?" asked a man next to him.

"Must have tried to escape," said another man.

"Don't be silly. It's Singapore, for goodness's sake," said a third. "People don't get shot by soldiers here. It only happens in Thailand or the Philippines."

"Yeah. You're right," said the first man.

"We can only guess," said Kuan Hee. "We'll know shortly."

"Maybe—some soldier's gun went off accidentally," said the third. "You read about it in the newspaper. Remember the CISCO guard at the checkpoint? Playing with his revolver?"

"Here comes a soldier. He's in a hurry," said the first.

"Look. The soldiers are gathering outside that room," said the first.

"I can't hear what they are saying," said the second man.

"They look disoriented," said the third.

"Yeah. Something bad must have happened," said Kuan Hee. "Someone must have gotten shot."

Kuan Hee looked at the other guys around him. A while ago, they were nonchalant. Now, fear showed in their faces and their tremulous voices. Yet, he wasn't fearful. He was adamant in his belief that no Singaporean would ever shoot another Singaporean in cold blood—not in his world anyway. Alas, he had subscribed to the wrong doctrine. He was part of that group of Singaporeans who had been lulled by many good years of government into thinking that evil would not find its way into government—not in Singapore anyway. He had plain forgotten about the three deadly sins of man—greed, lust and power. He wasn't a social creature; or else he could have made conversation with them to find out more about their background.

Where are the student leaders? Kuan Hee wondered. *Have they been captured? Have they also been detained in SAFTI?* His thoughts drifted back to his family. He was sure his mother was worried sick. First—his father, now he. *She doesn't know I'm here. How do I tell her? Will they let me call home? Has Lina told her what happened?* These were things that went through his mind.

"Dinner time, dinner time," shouted a soldier as he

walked past the dormitory. He and another soldier shoved takeaways in Styrofoam boxes through the window. Its occupants grabbed these and passed them around. The fragrant sesame oil smell told everyone what was inside—chicken rice, Singapore's Number One hawker food.

"Where's the water? How do we get water here?" one of them asked the soldier.

"Right behind, coming," came the reply.

Soon, a soldier wheeling cartons of mineral water came into view. With food and water in hand, the room's occupants sat down to dinner, making small conversation with one another as they ate. Army cooks went the way of the Dodo in the 1990s. That's when the armed forces realized Singaporeans weren't producing enough children to feed its national service. Gone too were the GD men—general duty soldiers who sprayed insecticide to keep the mosquitoes away, and the drivers. It was now either DIY or farmed out to contractors.

A soldier came to the window to collect the used food boxes.

"What was the commotion about," asked a man.

"What commotion?" said the soldier.

"You know, the shooting," said the man.

"Oh that," said the soldier. He looked around him. "An officer got shot."

"Protester shot him?" said another man.

"No, no—a major shot him," said the soldier.

"Why—" But before the second man could finish his sentence, the soldier had already left the window.

This was indeed news to the detainees. At once, the room woke up to an outpouring of views. Questions flew and theories were proffered. Everyone wanted to share; none remembered their fear. *Can be the officer refused to carry out an order*, thought Kuan Hee. *But, what is so serious about this defiance that warrants a shooting? Guard duty as punishment—that is plausible; certainly not a firing squad!*

Kuan Hee roused from sleep. He opened his eyes. It was dark outside. He couldn't tell the time—his iPhone was not with him. The rumbling of heavy vehicles from behind the dormitory faded away into the distance. He stretched his arm and sat against the wall. He wasn't used to the make-shift bed here—at home, the mattress was at least thirty centimetres thick. Here, bed was a blanket spread across the floor. And he was sitting between two bunks. He was too slow—others had laid claim to all available bunks in the room. He was a reticent chap—always the last to queue for a free goodie bag or go up the bus. Served him right—he deserved to sleep on the floor; in this world, it was first-come-first-served. But, if you called him a born loser, he would deny it vehemently. He would say he was merely taking his time, that there wasn't any need to hurry for such things.

It was Kuan Hee's second day in detention. He was getting restless. There were so many questions in his mind. As the minutes ticked by, more questions sprang up—*so many questions, not a single answer in sight*, he lamented. Promptly after a bare-bones breakfast, the detainees were marched to a large hall five blocks away. There they assembled with detainees from other blocks. *There has to be at least a hundred in the hall. There is no sign of Tim in the bobbing heads*, Kuan Hee thought. The detainees were subjected to some brainwashing speech. A major—close-cropped hair, brawny, and towering over the stage—delivered an impassioned oratory about toeing the line—co-operating with the army. Major David Foo—that's what he had said his name was—then flashed a sardonic grin.

The only part of his speech that all or most of the detainees paid attention to was he inviting them to enjoy the surroundings for the few days. He said he was giving them plenty of time to think about their actions the previous day. He also dispatched a warning: that if they persisted in their errant ways, they would not get to see the light of day for months, perhaps years.

That parting shot dug into the hearts of the detainees. They sat up at once, taking in the seriousness of the message. The major's facial expression showed he minced no words. *Is he the major who shot the officer yesterday?* thought Kuan Hee. He could hazard a guess; his guess would turn out right.

CHAPTER 3

It was the third day of detention. But Kuan Hee hadn't been in detention for too long to lose sight of what day it was today—Sunday. In these few days, while the others in the room had become chums, he remained aloof, sticking to mere formalities such as saying thank you when someone passed a box of food. *Drat the pesky mosquitoes,* he thought, nursing his sore arms and legs. They had feasted on him the last few days.

This morning, the barracks was a hive of activity. The detainees heard the rumbling of vehicles. Then, some buses rolled into the compound. A soldier unlocked the dormitory doors and shouted for its occupants to gather in the square. There they were told to retrieve their belongings, then they were ordered to board the buses. They packed into the buses which dispatched them to where they had picked them up and promptly unloaded them there.

Once they alighted from the buses, the former detainees quickened their paces and fanned out in different directions. Kuan Hee reached for his iPhone. They were not allowed to use the phone on the bus. Alas. Its battery had gone flat. There were no public phones in this day and age—everyone had a smartphone—even the cleaning auntie. He could not call home; neither could he phone Lina. He looked around. Tim was not in sight. He dragged himself into the Orchard MRT Station and headed home. He had not gotten a good rest the last few days. He sank into a seat, oblivious to the goings-on.

There was not a soldier in sight outside Hougang MRT Station. People were moving around doing their own things. He hurried across the field, up Jalan Naung and came to his house. The family car was in the car park—Mum was at home. He pressed the control to open the gate. As it glided sideways, the front door opened and who was standing there?—his father and mother. Both were wearing anxious looks; they rushed out to hug him. His mother kissed him all over his face. They had so many questions.

"Where did they take you to?"

"Did you eat well?"

"Why didn't you call back? Did you sleep well?"

"Lina said they manhandled you; are you alright?"

"Are you injured?"

"Why are there mosquito bite marks on your arms—and your legs too?"

"You didn't shaved. Your clothes are smelly. Did you bathe the past few days?"

"We were worried sick," said his mother.

"We looked all over for you," said his father.

"We lodged reports at the police station," said his mother.

"I asked around at the Ministry of Defence," said his father. "But, nobody knew the answer. My friends there are in the dark about the coup. Only a select few had knowledge of it."

In the living room, his mother brought a glass of Coke—his favourite drink, and sat next to him. His father was across the coffee table, taking a good long look at him.

It was now his turn to ask questions.

"Dad, when did you come back?"

"They let us go home yesterday evening. I thought everything was fine at home till your mother told me something had happened to you."

"Did they ill-treat you?"

"No, Dad. But they locked us up in the dormitory."

"Whereabouts is this place?"

"SAFTI—where I did my BMT."

"Did they torture you?"

"No, Mum—nothing like that. But, they did try to give us a pep talk—obeying the military and all that."

"Dad, Mum, I was thinking about you all the time I was in there. I was worried that with you—Dad—and me under lock and key, Mum would have a breakdown."

"Dear me—dear me."

"It's over now, Kuan Hee. All over now. Don't fret."

"Lina called me last night. She was hysterical. Said she was afraid something bad might have happened to you."

"I'll call her afterwards. I'll meet up with her later."

"Oh, I forgot—Tim called too."

"Tim? Has he been released? I couldn't find him. I thought he was still in detention."

"It seems he managed to escape when the soldiers weren't paying attention to him. He wasn't captured."

"Gosh. He's so lucky. I mean, thank God he is OK. No wonder there was no sign of him at SAFTI."

"I'm glad you're home safe and sound, Kuan Hee."

"Don't worry, Mum. I'm fine—really."

With his iPhone fully charged, Kuan Hee was ready to meet Lina and Tim. They had arranged to be at Kovan MRT Station at 2:00 p.m.

Lina practically flew into Kuan Hee's arms. He was unaccustomed to such open displays of emotions. But, it was curious. Both had known each other since primary school days. He had to have known she had a thing for him.

"Wah, Lina—Lina. There are people here." He tried to get her arms off him, but in vain. Then, he gave up trying. She was emotion-packed. *It is good for her to let her frustrations out*, he thought.

"Who cares? I misssss you so, Kuan Hee—so much."

"Okay—Okay."

"You have lost weight, Kuan Hee."

"He hasn't, Lina—he still looks the same."

"Nope. He's much thinner."

"Kuan Hee, I'm envious of you—no kidding."

"Sorry, Tim—Tim, how did you manage to escape?"

"Long story. Let's get into the MRT station first. It's bloody hot out here."

When the threesome were properly seated and hydrated in McDonald's restaurant at NEX Shopping Mall, Tim shared his story.

"After we were separated, they took me to Lucky Plaza, where a struggle broke out between some of the soldiers and the guy who was speaking over the public address system. His supporters crowded around the soldiers who threatened to shoot—but they didn't dare."

Tim paused, and, waving his arms in front of him, mimicked the soldiers pointing their rifles at the protesters. Then he continued.

"So the crowd became bolder and attacked the soldiers. There was only a handful of soldiers—all enlistees, but there were so many protesters. They overwhelmed the soldiers. That's the time I made my getaway, together with some others."

"*Wah*. So brave of you, Tim."

"So lucky."

"In the end, did the guy get caught?"

"No, Kuan Hee. Tim said he escaped too."

"Yes. Take a look at channelsingapore.com. It says here that this guy—his name is Patrick Teo—is planning another big demonstration in Dhoby Ghaut. That's where the Istana is."

"Shall we go there to give our support?"

"Kuan Hee, for goodness's sake, you just got out of a jam. It's time to lie low."

"Lina, I may be timid, but I am certainly not a coward."

"Yeah, Lina. Kuan Hee's right. Our future is at stake. If we do nothing, we are helping this Colonel Tee stay in power."

"OK. But—next time, when there's trouble, don't ask me to leave you—because I won't."

"Aw. There won't be a next time. Promise."

"Here's an update on the Website. The opposition parties are attending the demonstration too."

"What parties?"

"First People's Party, One Singapore Party and Unity Party."

"What about the Green Party?"

"There's nothing on it. Perhaps, with the party's ministers in detention, they are without a head. So, can't decide."

"Possible. Possible."

"Kuan Hee, are we going to just watch the show or participate actively?

"It's a good time to start being proactive. What you think, Tim?"

"Agree a hundred percent."

"Let's do it!" said all in unison.

CHAPTER 4

That evening, Kuan Hee's father came into his room right after dinner. He appeared troubled. He seemed to have a lot of things that he wanted to say to him. His father grabbed a chair and motioned him to be seated; then he sat on the bed. Father and son started their heart-to-heart talk.

"I have a foreboding—of worse things to come in our way."

"Why, Dad? We're both home safely."

"Son—there are some things I'm going to tell you now that I want no one else to hear of."

"Mum?"

"Not even Mum."

"Why Dad?"

"For her own safety. And—she might not agree with my idea."

"I'm all ears, Dad."

"You know I have been doing research for the government for many years."

"Yes, Dad."

"You know I specialize in nanotechnology."

"Mmm."

"But, what you don't know—is that this is top secret

work. For the past ten years, I have been experimenting with the idea of transferring memories. First—in animals. Then in human beings."

"You mean, cut open the skull, remove the brain and transplant it in another person's skull?"

"No…No—not that. You are now studying nanotechnology in electronic devices, right?" To this, Kuan Hee nodded.

"In a nutshell, it's about transferring the memories housed in electrical circuits—in this case the synapses in the human brain which are actually electrical in nature—to synapses in another brain."

"You mean—there's no need for any operation?"

"No…No. That's not it. A minor operation is needed. Just to implant electrodes on the skull, but these won't be visible as they are very small, and will be covered by the person's hair."

"I see. What you are doing is simply duplicating the brain's electromagnetic currents and copying them onto the synapses in another brain."

"Yes, Kuan Hee. Something like that—but, it's much more complicated than what you have explained."

"Have you succeeded, Dad?"

"More or less. We just need a living human specimen to use as a prototype for our experiment."

"You mean—you need a guinea pig, Dad."

"Yes—but that's a rather crude name you have used."

"Gee, Dad, It's something out of a sci-fi movie."

"Yes, but it is now a reality—not something that may be possible in ten—twenty years' time."

"Mmm."

"Another experiment—this one is a possibility, but is not feasible, as yet."

"What's that?"

"I'm looking at cloning of human beings—not human parts or organs, but entire human beings."

"Wow. That's like fantasy, Dad."

"Kuan Hee, it's not fantasy—fantasy means NEVER possible. This is science fiction—meaning technology has advanced to such a stage that it can happen—though not so soon."

"I see, Dad."

"To be specific—I'm looking at clones reproducing clones perpetually, just like us human beings giving birth and ensuring the survival of our species."

"That's real deep, Dad. I can't begin to fathom the complex electronic sequencing that needs to be coded to replicate so many different memories in one person."

"Yes, son—that's why people like me are a rare breed—that's why we are important to the government."

"Is that why you were detained?"

"No. No—son, I wasn't detained. I was only being protected."

"Protected? That's a strange way of protecting someone."

"You see—the military is afraid some people may want to get their hands on us scientists. That's why they implemented the shutdown at my workplace."

"I see."

"But—that's not why we're having this talk, son."

"Mmmm."

"I'm concerned about the near future. The new guys in charge of the military—and of course the country—may be greedy people. They may want to get their hands on this technology."

"Why? It belongs to the whole country."

"To be specific—they may want to use it for their own selfish purposes."

"You mean—they want to replicate themselves?"

"Mmm. Not quite so, but something like that."

"That's mean—real mean."

"Yes, son. For this reason, I fear—I fear they may keep me under lock and key so they can use my skills."

"Can't you resign, Dad?"

"Even if I resign, they can still get to me."

"Can't we run away?"

"We can—but where can we hide? Your mum and I are no longer young. I'm already past seventy."

"What do you want me to do, Dad?"

"Listen carefully, son. They may come to get me any time, but before they do, I want us to be able to communicate with each other any time anywhere no matter how far apart we are."

"You're not making sense, Dad."

"I mean—I want to implant a nano-electronic communication device in you and also in me—so that we can talk to each other whenever we want."

"Is that possible? I thought it's sci-fi, Dad."

"It's now reality, son. Come, follow me."

Father and son climbed down the stairs, went past the living room into the study. His father stopped in front of the floor-to-ceiling bookshelf which stood at the far end of the room.

"Go get a ladder, Kuan Hee."

"The tall one or the short one?"

"Either one will do."

Kuan Hee returned quickly with a short ladder.

"Here, give me a hand, Kuan Hee. Move the large blue and white vase aside."

Once the vase was in a new position, Kuan Hee's father placed the ladder against the bookcase, climbed a few steps and reached for the end panel of the bookcase. He pressed twice on the panel and it slid open, revealing a knob. Then, he turned the knob and the bookcase rolled sideways, exposing an opening wide enough for two persons to enter.

"Come follow me down."

He turned on a switch at the start of the stairs. Below, the cellar was not much different from those Kuan Hee had seen in the movies, only this one was under his house—and, he had no idea it existed. The cellar was slightly smaller than their living room. In it were three cupboards at one end, two chairs and a table in the centre. There were two standing fans. The room was stuffy, but the ventilation seemed to improve as the minutes wore on. Then, the room began to feel cool.

"Does Mum know about this room?"

"Of course, she does."

"Has she been down here?"

"A few times—but she doesn't like the place because of the poor ventilation. You know your mum can't stand stale air."

"Mmm."

His father took out a thin box—the size of a pencil box—and opened it. There were about a dozen tiny electronic devices—each the size of a nano SIM card—the type used in mobile phones in the early noughties.

"I just need to embed this in your arm and my arm too, and we can communicate with each other."

"How? How do we connect the earphones and the microphone?'

"We don't need these."

"Ha?"

"We communicate via brainwaves."

"Really, Dad?"

"No kidding, son. When you get a cut, you feel pain. That's because the affected tissue sends distress signals to the brain. This device uses the same route to the brain."

"Wow. So cool."

"Yes, it is—isn't it?"

"You mean, I put one of these tiny things in my body and I can talk to you? How do I know you are listening?"

"When you say 'Logon Alpha', you are connected instantly. I'll hear your voice instantly. I'll hear whatever you say."

"How do I turn it off?"

"Simply end your call with 'Ten Four Alpha'."

"What if I'm asleep, Dad?"

"If I do not hear your voice, I'll try again another time."

"You can leave a message, can't you, Dad?"

"No—it doesn't work that way—there's no inbox. Everything is done on the fly."

"Do we use the same codes?"

"Yes, it's sort of like a walkie-talkie. It can't communicate with other devices."

"Really cool, man—I mean, really cool gadget."

"Now comes the difficult part."

"What?"

"You can't tell your mother about this."

"Why not?"

"She will never accept the idea of an electronic device being implanted in you."

"Don't worry—Mum's the word."

"Hahaha, Kuan Hee. You certainly are funny."

"Dad, for the gadget to work—is there a limit to the distance between us?"

"This little thing makes use of a satellite up there. So, theoretically, there's no limit."

"Wow."

"One more question—can it penetrate thick walls?"

"Never a problem."

"That's great, Dad."

"Kuan Hee, can we put this on now?"

"Sure Dad."

"Thank you, son. It won't be very painful—just an ant's bite."

Kuan Hee's father put on surgical gloves, swabbed some alcohol onto Kuan Hee's upper arm, and applied a cream onto the area. Next, he proceeded to implant the nano device in it. As his father had said, the procedure was almost painless—just an ant's bite.

"The slit in your skin will heal in a week. You won't see any scars."

"How about you, Dad?"

"Oh, mine is already in the arm." His father rolled up a sleeve to show Kuan Hee his upper arm. It was true—there wasn't any mark on it.

His father opened a metal cabinet behind him. There were two toy soldiers and a toy tank on a shelf. Next to them was a small box. One by one, he placed them on the table.

"Kuan Hee, meet Alex and Xander, my two favourite *Kakis*."

"They are so cool, Dad."

"Yes, they are, aren't they."

"It's all AI. They have the same motor skills that you have. Plus, they can think—unlike most other robots."

"I thought it's only make-believe stuff."

"No, son. It's real, alright."

"Alex and Xander—show what you can do." The two robots did some somersaults and sparred with each other."

"Can they talk?"

"They can—but I have disabled that feature—it's not necessary, in my view."

"Where's the remote control, Dad?"

"What? Oh, there's no need for remotes. These two are not like the robots you see in the stores—you see, they can think."

"They can think? You mean, like us?"

"Yes, they are very advanced robots—the state of the art."

"Wow."

"You only need to tell them what you want to do, and they will oblige."

"Will they go against us?"

"Nope. These are kind robots—they don't do evil."

"Can I try giving commands, Dad?"

"Go ahead, son."

Kuan Hee had a smashing good time playing with Alex and Xander.

"If we are away from them, and need to communicate

with them, we phone them—They are linked to a satellite. By the way, they each have their own telephone number."

"Not using the Internet, like the appliances in the house?"

"No, that's rather archaic. The Internet of Things is an obsolete technology—in my eyes, anyway."

"How do we charge them when they run out of power?"

"No need, son. You see, they run on solar energy and they have a reserve store built into them—but, you have to bring them out once in a while to soak in the sunlight."

Next, his father opened the small box and took out two metal insect robots—a dragonfly and a large housefly.

"These little insects are your eyes in the sky. They are like the aerial drones that you see everywhere."

"They are so small, Dad."

"But—they pack a punch."

"How do we call them to give instructions?"

"We don't. Here are the remotes." His father handed him two cards—the size of credit cards. He unfolded each one to reveal a screen on one side and control buttons on the other."

"And these run on solar power, too?"

"Yes—they also have night vision capability."

"Wow. That's a nifty feature—and they are so small."

"Nano technology, son—state of the art—when you have time, take them for a spin—but, avoid places where there are people."

"I know, Dad."

"You know how to get inside this place. Come in whenever you want."

"Mum? Should I keep them a secret from Mum?"

"Hahaha. No need, son. She knows about my little toys."

"Thanks, Dad. I'll take good care of them."

"I know you will. Remember—these are powerful

tools. Don't intrude into others' privacy—unnecessarily."

"Trust me, Dad."

"I have placed the tools in your hands. The rest is up to you, son."

"Ha?"

CHAPTER 5

By the time they arrived at Dhoby Ghaut MRT Station, it was jam-packed with people, all jostling and shoving to get out of the station. Tim was in front, with Lina behind him, and Kuan Hee at the tail end, holding on to Lina's arms. Together, their little train weaved through the crowd out onto the walkway.

Every which way the looked, there were people. It was indeed a big demonstration, the likes of which the trio had not seen. It was late afternoon, and the sweltering June heat was taking its toll on the demonstrators. There were volunteers making their rounds, passing out bottles of water. Some protesters had set up small tents on the road—there were no cars or buses; apparently the burgeoning human traffic had vehicles stopped in their tracks, whether on Orchard Road itself, along Dhoby Ghaut or Bras Basah, all the way south to Victoria Street.

There was virtually no way any army could contain the protesters. It was a sea of people—young and old, wheel-chair-bound, stroller-walking, placard-holding, loud-hailer-wielding; all were chanting slogans in unison.

At the appointed time, speaker by speaker from different political parties, gathering on a small make-shift platform in front of the Cathay Building, moved up to say their piece in support of the movement to protest against the coup. They called for Colonel Tee to step down and return power to the rightful elected government. Their voices blared through speakers mounted on the roadside. Patrick Teo, leader of the protesters in Orchard Road was the last to speak. He was a firebrand. His words arouse the patriotic spirit in the audience who chanted pro-democracy slogans. It was indeed a strange sight—for Singaporeans were unaccustomed to such vocal displays of support.

Kuan Hee, Tim and Lina raised their arms in rhythm with others around them. They too chanted slogans. It was one Singapore voice reverberating across the entire city area. Then came alarm, which descended into chaos— Someone or some people had thrown Molotov cocktails onto the stage. There were screams—Patrick Teo had taken a direct hit; he was instantly set ablaze. Some on stage beat flames off their shirts and pants; some took cover behind chairs. Others jumped into the crowd below. From where they were standing, the trio could make out some protesters wrestling with two men. They pinned them to the ground. On stage, some people were carrying a darkened figure—*Is it Patrick Teo?* thought Kuan Hee— off the stage. The remaining people on stage gathered next to the microphone.

A voice over the loudspeakers urged calm. It appealed to everyone not to panic. It took some minutes before the pandemonium subsided, and order set in. Ambulance paramedics were on hand at the front of Capitol Building to attend to the injured. But, that was all they could do. There was no way their ambulance could move from its spot—there were people everywhere.

As darkness fell, the crowd grew thinner. It was past dinner time and many had yet to fill their stomachs. They were inexperienced in attending protests, so they came unprepared for the long haul. They had thought that it was just like attending a political rally speech at election time, after which they could disperse. Here, the organisers were cajoling them to stay—for the night, at the very least, or better still, till tomorrow. But, this was not Hong Kong. Here, people were still not ready to brave the elements for days for a good cause; here, people were pragmatic—bread and butter was the only important thing to them, at least for now. They would need more convincing before deciding to dig in their heels with the protest leaders.

The threesome thought the spot outside MacDonald's House they had picked was safe as it was not near the speakers' platform. But, they were in for a rude shock. A backpack that someone had left behind exploded near them. The impact threw all three to the ground. Kuan Hee quickly rolled to Lina and wrapped himself over her. Tim tried to push himself up but fell. The boys looked up. There were dust and debris around them. People were caked in dust. Some were screaming from pain; others were crying. The three of them were lucky to escape with scrapes and bruises, but the scene was ugly. There were mangled bodies; body parts were strewn on the roadside. Several people were injured by shrapnel from the bomb. Nails could be seen on the road. Apparently, the bomb was constructed to inflict maximum damage.

In the ensuing chaos, some stomped on others, while some others stumbled on the fallen. Policemen and paramedics were trying to get to the injured, but it was a painstakingly slow process—there were too many people congregating here. The explosion outside the MacDonald's House in Orchard Road put paid to the idea of staying on in the area. Kuan Hee and company decided to call it a day as it was too risky now; they could become the next victims. There was no knowing when and where the next strike would take place. It was better to be safe than sorry. The crowd apparently felt the same way, for waves of people were seen moving slowly towards the peripheral roads, away from the main protest area.

Watching the 9:00 p.m. news in the safety of his home, Kuan Hee heard the news presenter describing the demonstration in Dhoby Ghaut as a failure. She reported that terrorists had infiltrated the demonstration site. *What a laugh*, Kuan Hee thought. The presenter said they were responsible for the explosions which killed six people, including a protest leader named Patrick Teo; and injured scores of others. She urged people, for their own safety, not to attend protests.

An hour later, an army spokesman appeared on a special news bulletin. He announced the setting up of a new council named National Reconciliation Council which, he said, had authorized the dissolution of parliament. Next, he said that the NRC had vested its power in the Supreme Leader of the Council who would act as Prime Minister till elections were held. Last, he introduced the members of the NRC. Heading the list was Supreme Leader Colonel Tee, with Major Warren Tan named as Deputy Supreme Leader, and Major David Foo as Secretary-General. According to him, the President had given his assent to the appointments.

Kuan Hee, having received military training not too long ago, and, therefore, was acquainted with the military hierarchy, laughed. He scoffed at the announcements. *Fancy putting themselves above the generals in the army, navy and air forces; what a laugh*, he thought.

It was to be a long night of announcements. At 10:30 p.m., the army spokesman reappeared on national television. He said that in the interest of national security, the leaders of several political parties had been detained under the Internal Security Act. He gave no other information.

Kuan Hee heard the rattling of the gate as it rolled to the side. His father and mother were back.

"Hi Dad and Mum."

"Have you taken dinner, dear?"

"Fried rice, Mum."

"Again?"

"Yes, Mum. I needed something that would fill my stomach. I didn't eat much in the afternoon."

"Is that a special announcement on TV?"

"Yes, Dad. The army has formally dissolved parliament."

"I was wondering when they would come around to doing it."

"Dad, are we under martial law?"

"No, Kuan Hee. We are under military rule, not martial law—not yet anyway."

"Does it mean—we have lost our freedom?"

"The short answer?—Yes. And some friends of mine in government have disappeared overnight."

"Disappeared? As in—missing?"

"Yes, I'm afraid so. No one knows where they are. A likely guess would be some army camp."

"Like, in my case?"

"Yes. And the police are powerless. Some of its top brass have been transferred to project work. There's nobody running the police force presently."

"Dad, why are the coup leaders doing these things?"

"To silence dissent, of course."

"But, if you remove talented people, how do you run the country effectively?"

"They have no interest in that. What they want is to hold on to power. So, they are suspicious of everyone."

"Including the newspapers?"

"They need a tame press. So, they bully the media into compliance with their instructions."

"But—they are destroying Singapore, Dad."

"They don't care; they are obsessed with power—getting it and keeping it."

"Does it also mean there will be no elections from now on?"

"I think so, son. Elections are a no-no to dictators."

"But, just now, the presenter was saying something

about the NRC running the country till elections are held."

"Well, son. These are outright lies—said to appease people. They will come up with new excuses to delay holding elections—for sure."

"Dear, it's bedtime. You have classes tomorrow."

"OK Mum. Thanks Dad, for sharing."

"No problem, son."

"Son, remember—no one can cling on to power forever. The history books have numerous examples of fallen dictators."

"Yes, Dad. Goodnight, Mum and Dad."

CHAPTER 6

The long overpass which stretched into Temasek University was crowded with students this morning. Some soldiers manning the gate were checking students one by one as they passed through the gate. They were scanning matriculation cards into portable terminals. *Are they looking for certain students?* Kuan Hee wondered, *or are they merely taking attendance?* He and Lina were allowed in after their bags were checked.

There was a buzz on the fifth storey, outside their EEE classroom. Fellow classmates were exchanging pointers; they seemed to be discussing some important matter.

"What's up, Navin?" asked Kuan Hee.

"Kuan Hee, you are here—Mr Lee has been taken away by some soldiers," said Navin.

"S-e-r-i-o-u-s?" said Lina.

"Yeah. And for no rhyme or reason," said Navin.

"That's bad news. Are the other lecturers alright?" said Lina.

"I asked the programme officer. She said he's the only one. All his classes have been cancelled," said Navin.

"I hear Mr Lee belongs to the Unity Party. Someone

said he was one of those behind the Dhoby Ghaut demonstration," said a student.

"Look. Jordan is here—he's being escorted by two guys," said another student. The students turned their heads in the direction of the lift lobby.

"Hi. Everyone," said Jordan. His two burly escorts walked towards the opposite classroom and stood there.

"Why the fancy escorts?" asked Navin.

"Let's not talk about them," said Jordan, shaking his head. Pointing to the escorts, he continued, "There goes my freedom."

"You mean they follow you everywhere?" said Lina.

"Yeah. Even the toilets," said Jordan.

"Who are they? They look menacing," said Kuan Hee.

"Army guys," came the reply.

'Are you under detention?" asked Lina.

"Lina, how can he be under detention when he is walking around freely?" said Tim. He had just arrived and heard the conversation.

"Or is he under house arrest?" said Lina.

"Aiyoh, Lina. You are a pain—" said Tim.

"Don't be mean to her," said Kuan Hee. "Lina, they are Jordan's bodyguards."

"*Wah*. Really?" said the rest in unison.

"*Wah seh*. Is his father a millionaire?" said Navin.

"Jordan, is your father rich?" said Lina.

"Nah. These are my father's people," said Jordan. "He sent them to protect me."

"Then, your family must be rich," said Lina.

"You guys are very *kaypoh*," said Jordan. "Everything you also want to know."

"Tell us *leh*, Jordan," said Navin.

"Alright—alright," said Jordan. "My father is Tee Bak Chai."

"Who?" said Lina.

"Hah? Doesn't ring a bell," said Navin.

"Is he some tycoon?" said Tim.

"He's Colonel Tee—the Supreme Leader of NRC," said Tim.

"Gosh—the dictator," said Lina.

"Don't call my father a dictator!" said Jordan. He contorted his eyebrows and stared at Lina.

"Let's not quarrel," said Kuan Hee. "We're all friends, man."

"She started it all," said Jordan.

"Since class has been cancelled, let's go down to the cafeteria for a drink," said Kuan Hee. "My treat." He herded the group towards the lift lobby. The two bodyguards followed them.

In the cafeteria, the five of them crammed at a small table next to the clear glass panels overlooking the car park. The bodyguards sat at the next table. The air-conditioning seemed ineffective in cooling Lina and Jordan down. Kuan Hee started the ball rolling.

"Guys, give me your orders," said Kuan Hee.

"Are these guys going to tell your father what we are talking about?" said Kuan Hee when he returned with a tray of drinks.

"They won't dare," said Jordan. "I won't let them."

"Jordan, you are the deputy student leader," said Navin. "Won't you be at loggerheads with your dad?"

"He is he and I am I," came the reply.

"Kuan Hee, won't there be a conflict of interest? Father—Supreme Leader, and son—a deputy student leader?" asked Navin.

"Aiyah. We are merely student representatives—no big deal, lah," said Kuan Hee. "It's not like he's a supreme court judge and his father is Supreme Leader."

"Kuan Hee's right," said Tim. "Lina, don't you agree—Lina?"

"Don't be a spoilsport, Lina," said Kuan Hee. Lina glared at him.

"Jordan," said Kuan Hee. "Why is your father doing

this—taking over the country?"

"Yeah, why?" said Tim and Navin in unison.

"I don't know. I'm angry with him too," said Jordan. "I haven't talked to him in days—I can't understand why he is so power crazy."

"You mean, you don't agree with his actions?" said Lina. Hearing his remarks, she became her usual self again.

"I hear you guys went to the big demonstration," said Jordan. "I hear you took a hit."

"Nah. Just some minor bruises, that's all," said Kuan Hee.

"Here, look," said Tim, sticking out a leg and pointing at it.

"Sorry, so sorry," said Jordan.

"It's not your fault, Jordan," said Kuan Hee.

"Is this your father's work?" said Tim.

"I—" said Jordan, craning his neck to get a look at the next table. His bodyguards were stirring their cuppa. "I overheard my father saying something in the study."

"What is it, Jordan?" said Kuan Hee. "You can trust us. We won't tell a soul."

"We won't. We won't," the others said in unison.

The others hunched around him. His voice had softened into a whisper and they wanted to hear what he was saying.

"My father—he could be behind the explosion," said Jordan.

"What?" exclaimed Navin.

"Shhh!" said the others in unison. The bodyguards turned their heads in the direction of the students, and resumed sipping their cuppa.

"S-e-r-i-o-u-s?" said Tim.

"Your father gave the order for the explosion?" said Navin.

"Yes," said Jordan.

"And the Molotov cocktail throwers—he sent them?" said Tim.

"Yes," said Jordan.

"*Wah Lau*. People died—you know," said Lina.

"Yeah. And we were almost killed," said Tim.

"I'm sorry about it—very sorry," said Jordan. "But, I am helpless. He—just won't listen to me."

"What about your mother?" asked Lina.

"She—she's behind him all the way," said Jordan.

"Your mother, too?" said Kuan Hee.

"I asked her why—she said he worked so hard; yet he's only a colonel."

"Isn't being a colonel good enough?" said Navin. "I don't think I can even make the grade—if I try."

"My father is—an A-level holder. He didn't go to university," said Jordan. "I'm the first one to enter university."

"I see," said Kuan Hee. "I see."

"Aren't you going to try talking to him again?" said Lina.

"No use, Lina—no use," said Jordan.

"Does your father know you are a student leader?" said Kuan Hee.

"Nope," came the reply.

"Are you not going to tell him?" said Navin. Jordan was silent on this.

"Let's not push him," said Kuan Hee. "Let's drop the topic."

"Yeah. Let's talk about other things," said Lina. From the tone of his voice, she could sense Jordan's spirits sagging.

WHATSAPP:
"URGENT meeting @ open space outside EEE, 11:00 a.m. today," texted Donald Chen.

"Guys, I've got to attend a students' union meeting now," said Kuan Hee.

"Me too," said Jordan.

"Kuan Hee, I'll wait for you here," said Lina.

"Same," said Tim.

"What about your bodyguards, Jordan?" asked Kuan Hee. "We can't bring them along, you know—it's going to be about the military takeover."

"Not to worry," said Jordan. "I'll tell them to stay clear of the place."

The secretary of the Temasek University Students' Union had convened a meeting of student leaders from different faculties in the university. It was meant to discuss a soft protest along the Singapore River. The focal point of the protest was the stretch of river behind the Parliament Building. The proposal was for students from the six local universities to hold a candlelight vigil, significantly to mourn the death of democracy, and specifically to protest the dissolution of parliament and curtailment of freedom to assemble in Singapore. The NRC had announced that assemblies of six or more people were illegal and those who participated in such assemblies risked arrest.

The candlelight vigil was held to intentionally signal to the coup leaders that the students were not afraid to violate the assembly order to fight for their cause. A total of 30,000 students were expected to attend the night event which would be held on the evening of National Day itself.

Temasek University's students would occupy the stretch of river from Cavenagh Bridge to Empress Place. The organisers forecasted the event would end very late at night and said participants could leave for home on the first MRT train or bus in the area which would start running at 5:45 a.m.

CHAPTER 7

It was 9 August 2030. Today was National Day, but celebrations were far from the minds of locals. A few days ago, the military had held a rehearsal for the National Day parade at The Float, a large metal platform the size of a football field, floating next to the banks of Marina Bay. Its seating gallery had a capacity of 30,000 people. The parade was quickly put together by the army which ordered participants of the Youth Festival in June to reprise their performances for the parade.

The parade would start at 6:00 p.m. By 10:00 a.m., the entire area stretching from St Andrew's Road, Connaught Drive and Beach Road to Raffles Avenue and Raffles Boulevard had been cordoned off. Armored personnel carriers guarded the junctions of these roads. There were army soldiers scurrying around, making preparations for the parade.

The university students' candlelight vigil would stretch from the mouth of the Singapore River to Clarke Quay. As the two venues were close to each other, there was a high possibility of a clash between the soldiers and the students. Perhaps, the students had intentionally chosen the river site to stage their soft protest. Perhaps, the students would march towards the parade zone in a vehement show of force. Perhaps, the military would fire at the protesters. There was no answer to these questions—yet.

The threesome arrived early outside Raffles Place MRT Station. Kuan Hee had delegated some administrative work to his two pals. He was in charge of distributing candles and water to participants. The truck carrying cartons of the water had dropped its load at the open area next to Emplace Place. Metres away, there was a chain of soldiers blocking access to St Andrew's Road, where City Hall building was. They were backed by two armored personnel carriers. Some police vans and buses had also arrived; these were parked along St Andrew's Road. Policemen bearing shields disembarked and moved in a single file towards the protest area. The line between the military coup leaders and their detractors was becoming denser.

This was Kuan Hee's first active participation in a protest. Now he wasn't a bystander; he was a bona fide student leader, with followers who would look up to him to set examples for them. Now, he was an activist, but he wasn't a firebrand like Patrick Teo. Maybe this was why Patrick Teo was in the netherworld, and he, on earth. He had yet to kindle the fire within him. It would take more than just the threat of a jobless future to wake the activist in him—In his mind, the future was still far away. Perhaps, if Lina was hurt; perhaps, if his father or mother was in danger. Perhaps, if he was staring at death in the face.

What did Kuan Hee know about being a leader? He was an only child—with no brothers or sisters to hover over him or quarrel with. His mother gave birth to him when she was forty-five years old. At that age it was too risky, so they settled for caesarean delivery. He was a mummy's boy then; he was still a mummy's boy now.

"Kuan Hee, where are the lighters for the candles?" asked Lina.

"Jordan and Navin will be bringing them here. They are

collecting them from Donald now."

News of the candlelight vigil event spread like wildfire on social media. There were numerous comments on Facebook and Twitter. Within hours, thousands swarmed into the Marina area. *They are going the wrong way—the parade is in the opposite direction!* thought soldiers stationed at the checkpoints. These people were here to lend support to the students; they were not attending the parade. The crowds overwhelmed the soldiers. They surrounded the armored personnel carriers. In no time, the Padang was a sea of people. In the waning light, they were a large moving blob of heads. There were not enough candles to pass around to them. But, it didn't matter—they came prepared with their own. Singapore had its last major blackout back in the late 1970s and since then, people did not stock up on candles. How did these people get the candles? There probably weren't enough in the stores, if they could find them. Some others were ingenious—they used LED torches to light up the surroundings.

It was now dark everywhere; the street lamps had been turned off using IP commands. In the Internet of Things era, even street lamps had their own IPs. If the military could not stop the candlelight vigil, the least it could do without resorting to violence was to do as little as they could to help the protesters along. It soon appeared as if a swarm of fireflies had descended upon the area. Wave upon wave of flickering lights moving in an undulating manner lit up the Padang. Surveillance drones shone their lights onto the crowd.

There was blaring of music from The Float—The parade had started. Contingents of soldiers from the army, navy and the air force marched along the tarmac in front of the seating gallery. The police also had a contingent. There was a convoy of military and police vehicles in the procession. But, civilian participation was dismal. Gone were the usual contingents from the union, the telecom companies, the big MNCs and statutory boards. In their place were schoolchildren replaying their Youth Festival performances. The seating gallery was packed, but they were all uniformed staff. The military rule had gotten off to a bad start.

Over at the candlelight vigil, there were no speeches, unlike the protests in Dhoby Ghaut and Orchard Road. After the violence that marred the earlier protests, the organisers were now taking a different approach. Hopefully, tonight would pass without any incident, but it remained to be seen—for the night was still young.

Kuan Hee and company were now standing on Cavenagh Bridge; they had a good view of the river banks from this spot. So far, things had been running smoothly; except for a lost child, there wasn't anything to dampen their spirits.

A bodyguard tapped on Jordan's shoulder and whispered into his ear. Jordan followed him somewhere. He didn't tell Kuan Hee or the others. They thought he was leaving the protest. Then he returned.

"Sorry, guys. It was my father," said Jordan. "He wanted me to go home with him."

"I'm glad you didn't leave with him," said Tim.

"Yeah." The others chirped in unison.

"Jordan, the soldiers have left us alone tonight," said Kuan Hee. "Is it because you are here?"

"I doubt so," said Jordan. "My father couldn't care less about me." But his father's action contradicted this remark. After all, his father had taken the time to stop by to speak to him. And Jordan was his only child.

"Was Colonel Tee angry?" asked Lina.

"About me being here?" said Jordan.

"Nope—about people coming to our protest instead of heading to his parade," said Lina.

"Well, his face was glum," said Jordan. That remark said it all. Would Jordan's father take retaliatory action against the protesters? Nobody knew the answer, but it was plausible.

"Let's not talk about him," said Jordan.

It was almost 3:00 a.m. Many people who had joined the candlelight vigil had already left with their families. The river banks held only students and some others who wanted to enjoy one another's company in the early morning. The soldiers stood wearily on nearby St Andrew's Road. Donald then called a meeting of the student leaders. Apparently, some of them wanted to continue the protest into the morning and they had to get the others' concurrence. If only a handful of students were willing, the protest could not carry on—it would lack strength. Finally, everyone agreed to stay on. Then they mapped out what they needed to do once dawn broke. Their supplies had been depleted. They needed more water and food. Their phones and tablets were running out of juice; without a portable supply of electricity, their mission was bound to fail. And they also had to get more umbrellas; it was going to get hot come late morning.

Lina had permission to spend the night, but the next day was another thing. Her mother was asleep now; she had to wait till 5:30 a.m. when her mother would get up to go marketing. She wasn't sure she wanted to make the call. But, she also didn't want to go home alone. Kuan Hee was her world. She didn't want to leave him behind. The last time she did that—he went missing for a few days, and she couldn't sleep those few days.

As she pondered over the matter, she plain forgot time had not stood still. It was now 5:45 a.m. She had to make the call now. After some scoldings on the phone, her mother relented. She trusted Lina when she was in the company of Kuan Hee. Over the years, Kuan Hee had made frequent visits to their home, and her mother like what she saw—Here was a dependable chap, albeit on the soft side, not brawny like Lina's three brothers. He was the educated type, not like her brothers who didn't make it to polytechnic or junior college. Lina was her mother's hope—she was the only child who had made it to university. It wasn't difficult to support Lina through university as the brothers were all working. Their father had passed away when the children were young and their mother had to take on several jobs to feed the family. Hopefully, Lina could lean on Kuan Hee for company for the rest of her life.

At 7:00 a.m., two men came to take over the two who were guarding Jordan. They brought along breakfast for Jordan; it was prepared by his mother. There was enough to share with Kuan Hee and company. By now, only a tenth of the original student strength remained at the protest site. Many students who left had promised to return later in the day. They just had to report home to make their worried parents happy.

Over at the Padang, more soldiers were arriving; some to relieve the soldiers who had spent the night here; others to reinforce the numbers, in case the protest took an ugly turn. The police contingent left in their vehicles. Another two armored personnel carriers rumbled onto the Padang tarmac.

But the muted early morning was soon to turn chaotic, for the student leaders had decided to lead the students onto City Hall. It was something that the military would not turn a blind eye to. As more students poured into Empress Place, the protest leaders used loud hailers to cajole them into action. Kuan Hee and his pals were taken by surprise—they didn't expect to march to City Hall. It was a last-minute decision by some student leaders. Alas, they had no choice but to follow along. After all, they were part of the student movement. They had to be as gung-ho as the others on the heroic and praiseworthy goal of saving Singapore from the clutches of dictatorship. Yes, that was what Kuan Hee and his friends had to convince themselves.

Kuan Hee grabbed a loud hailer, so did Jordan. Together with Lina, Tim and Navin, they marched with students from the other universities to St Andrew's Road. But the soldiers were ready for them; there was a long chain of soldiers bearing rifles standing abreast in the middle of the wide road. This time, Kuan Hee's group was right in front of the procession. Their representative had drawn lots, and it was decided that Temasek University would take the lead. Donald, Jordan and Kuan Hee were in front; Lina, Tim and Navin were behind them. Tim and Navin were holding placards denouncing military rule. Jordan's bodyguards were directly behind Jordan; they were ready to pull Jordan to safety should things turn ugly. It seemed they were the only reluctant participants of the protest.

The crowd shouted slogans as they moved in step, drawing nearer to the City Hall steps, where the surrender of the Japanese forces had taken place in World War II. A voice boomed over the public address system across the Padang.

"Stop the protest and disperse immediately," the voice commanded. Soon, a jeep roared into view. The soldiers forming the chain moved aside to let it pass.

"Go home now and we will not take action against you," said the same voice. It belonged to a Captain who was standing on the jeep. He looked to be middle-aged.

The came the rumbling of heavy vehicles. Some trucks bearing water cannons appeared behind the jeep. They were police vehicles, but it was army personnel manning the trucks.

Where are the police? Kuan Hee and the others wondered.

The protesters refused to bulge and the army captain gave the order to use the water cannons against them, drenching them. The powerful jets of water fell some of them, but they got up again and relocked arms with one another. Kuan Hee and company were all wet; they were also cold, but they forced themselves to be strong. The bodyguards did not escape the drenching, but they remained in position behind Jordan. Next, some soldiers lobbed tear gas canisters into the crowd. The protesters tried hard to dodge these. As the canisters rolled on the tarmac, they emitted plumes of smoke which enveloped the protesters. People were coughing and wheezing; their eyes were tearing uncontrollably. Some vomited; others cried in pain. Some splashed water into their eyes; it made things worse. Some others covered their face with tissue paper, towel or whatever that was at hand. Kuan Hee and Jordan suffered the most as they were right in front. Poor Lina was tearing; she cried as the tear gas singed her eyes. The poor bodyguards were probably the only innocent victims in the whole affair. They covered their faces with handkerchiefs. The protesters were clearly unprepared for this latest strategy of the soldiers. For all of them, this was probably their first experience in a protest; for Singapore, it was the first time that soldiers were attacking civilians. History had been made, courtesy of the military.

There was a lull in the action as the captain had ordered his soldiers to take a break while he assessed the situation. It gave the students time to regroup and rethink strategies. Still searing from the tear gas attack, the students retreated a few metres till they were out of range of the projectiles. Some male students had now taken off their T-shirts or jerseys and were readying them to protect themselves against the tear gas canisters.

The lull was broken by a fresh volley of projectiles whizzing over the students. This time, the students were better prepared. The female students had retreated to the back of the procession, and T-shirt bearing protesters fended off the projectiles. One grabbed a canister and threw it back at the soldiers who winced in the smoke, for they too were unprepared for the tear gas attack. Another student mimicked the act. Some soldiers were seen stumbling onto the ground. Others fell onto their fellow soldiers. The captain's jeep was enveloped by tear gas. The captain coiled in despair; his eyes were smarting.

Clearly, both warring parties were incensed. The

students were petrified that the military had resorted to hardball tactics to deal with their peaceful protest. That quickly changed into anger. And the captain was indignant that the students were fighting back. Here he was trying to restore law and order in the streets; and there they were—fighting the law.

There was a flurry of action on the soldiers' side. The protesters heard the humming of engines. Then the armored personnel carriers sprang into action. They rumbled along the tarmac in front of the City Hall steps. It was to be a David versus Goliath fight—between the unarmed students and armored personnel carriers. Was it time for the students to run helter-skelter? What would the student leaders decide to do? Their lives, and those of their followers were at stake. How would the students' parents react if they knew what was happening?

It was now too late for second thoughts or decisions. The soldiers were not to be trifled with; it was either retreat or suffer defeat and injury for the protesters. Donald moved a few steps in front of the other protesters. He drew a deep breath and headed towards the armored personnel carriers. Soon he was within metres of the huge vehicles. Was he crazy, or was he fearless? What if the armored personnel carriers ran over him? He would become *roti prata!* Now the armored personnel carriers had stopped. The soldier on top of the front most armored personnel carrier was in two minds. *Should I run over the student, or should I keep still,* he thought. Undecided, he talked furiously into the headphones.

Jordan could not stand it any longer. He broke from the others and ran towards Donald. The bodyguards had no choice but to follow in pursuit. Kuan Hee did a strange thing. Timid Kuan Hee lunged after Jordan. The four of them were soon within metres of Donald. Alas. It was too late, for the armored personnel carrier lumbered along, over Donald and on towards Jordan and Kuan Hee. The two boys recoiled in horror. Their friend had been crushed under the tracks of the armored personnel carrier. They stopped in their tracks, then, recovering from the shock, they threw themselves against the front of the armored personnel carrier. The two bodyguards were talking furiously into their wireless communication devices; they were trying to get help for Jordan. The soldier atop the armored personnel carrier drew his gun and took aim at the two boys. Then he shot at them. One. Two. Three. There were three shots—one ricocheted upon hitting the front of the armored personnel carrier. Another hit Jordan's left leg. He let out a shrill cry. And a third struck Kuan Hee in his right arm. Kuan Hee grimaced in pain and fell off the armored personnel carrier onto the tarmac. He rolled in pain. A bodyguard helped him up and both hobbled away from the armored personnel carrier, towards the protesters. Another grabbed Jordan and followed them. The soldier on the armored personnel carrier trained his gun on them; he was about to shoot again. Suddenly his headphones crackled with new instructions and he put away his weapon.

Poor Lina. She saw the whole thing unfolding before her eyes. She was now wailing away. Her tears were unstoppable. It was like a well that had overflowed.

Not since the second world war had the City Hall building witnessed bloodshed. It was unprecedented in Singapore history—army soldiers firing at unarmed civilians.

CHAPTER 8

It was a two-bed ward that Kuan Hee and Jordan shared at Singapore General Hospital. Jordan's bodyguards were outside the doorway. His parents had yet to visit him. Kuan Hee's father and mother were seated by his side. Both wore anxious looks. Lina was standing next to Kuan Hee's mother. Tim was by the window.

"Mum, I'm sorry," said Kuan Hee.

"It's alright, dear," said his mother. She was grasping Kuan Hee's hand with one hand, and fingering his arm with the other.

"Is your arm still tender?" she asked. Kuan Hee nodded.

"Why didn't you tell us you were staying the night at Singapore River?" said his father.

"Sorry, Dad," said Kuan Hee, "I forgot." But, it was a lie. He didn't tell them as he was worried that they might not approve of his staying overnight at the river.

"I want you to resign as a student leader," said his father. "These army guys are not to be trifled with. This time you hurt your arm. Next time, it may cost you your life."

"Yes, Kuan Hee. Your father is right," said his mother.

"You should know your priorities. Studies come first."

"I want an answer," said his father.

Kuan Hee nodded in agreement. He had to pacify his parents now. He didn't want them to spend more sleepless nights worrying about him. He had to give a convenient, albeit untruthful answer. But, he would try to keep out of trouble for a while.

There were so many things that Lina wanted to say to Kuan Hee, but she couldn't. There were too many people in the ward. It would be awkward if she told him she almost died seeing him fall off the armored personnel carrier. She didn't care what Tim or Jordan would say. What would Kuan Hee's parents think of her? It was painful to keep her thoughts to herself, but she had no choice today.

"Don't worry, Mrs Wang," said Lina. "I'll keep an eye on him—make sure he doesn't get into trouble again."

A nurse came into the ward. Visiting hours were over and she told the visitors they could come again the next day. She waited as one by one they shuffled out of the room.

It was after visiting hours that they came. Bodyguards ushered Jordan's father and mother into the ward. Kuan Hee realized why his own father and mother, and his friends had been shooed out of the ward—VIPs were coming. It was the first time that Kuan Hee had seen Jordan's parents at close range. Colonel Tee looked no older than sixty. True to his army roots, he was tanned and had close cropped hair—albeit greying. His face was wizened. His forehead had crept into the place where his hair used to occupy. At first look, you were attracted to his bushy disheveled eyebrows. He spoke in a husky voice.

Jordan's mother looked like any auntie you met at the market. She was not the polished type you would see in high society. It was clear Jordan was her son—he took after her features. You could see her long face and bony cheeks in him; but, he had his father's small eyes. She, too, spoke in a soft tone.

Both Mr and Mrs Tee were thrifty with words in the ward. But, their long silence spoke volumes. Perhaps, they were not comfortable speaking their mind with a stranger in the room. To them, Kuan Hee was an unknown. But, they were polite enough to ask after Kuan Hee and wish him a quick recovery.

Colonel Tee and his wife were busy people. They didn't stay long. Once Mrs Tee was convinced that her son's injury were not life threatening, they left. His mother promised to come the next day.

It was the second day of Kuan Hee's stay in hospital when the twenty-somethings could talk freely. Kuan Hee's parents had left early; they had to attend a wedding.

"So, what's the buzz?" asked Jordan.

"There's nothing in the news on what happened at City Hall," said Tim. "The newspapers and TV only reported on the candlelight vigil in a terse statement."

"What?" said Jordan. "These army guys fired on us and nothing gets reported?"

"Yeah, that's true," said Lina. "The newspaper and TV stations have been gagged, I believe."

"But, it's all over the Facebook and Twitter," said Tim.

"Yeah, photos of the shooting have been uploaded onto Facebook," said Lina. "And, it's gone viral."

"Here, take a look," said Tim, thrusting his smartphone into Jordan's hand.

"Come, Kuan Hee, see mine," said Lina.

Both patients swiped, pinched and jabbed the screens as they perused news articles and social media posts on the smartphones.

"Look. You and Jordan are famous now," said Lina.

"Yeah, they are saying how brave both of you were," said Tim. "Fancy running headlong into an armored personnel carrier."

"Donald died a martyr," said Kuan Hee.

"Donald's actually the real brave one," said Jordan.

"He gave his life for freedom."

"Agree," said the others in unison.

"Where's the wake for Donald?" asked Kuan Hee.

"It seems they still have not released his body to his parents," said Tim.

"I still can't believe the army moved in on us," said Jordan.

"I still can't accept the newspapers keeping mum about it," said Lina.

"It's so surreal," said Kuan Hee. "Are we living in a vacuum under military rule?"

"See, people are ranting like crazy on Facebook," said Tim.

"You can stop some of the people some of the time, but you can't stop all of the people all of the time," said Kuan Hee.

"Wow. That's deep," said Lina, impressed.

"I seem to have heard that before," said Tim. "Some American saying, right? You changed the words right?"

"Yes, *lah*," said Kuan Hee.

"Why use 'stop', why not use 'fool' instead?" asked Jordan. "It's a more accurate word."

"I'm glad we have Websites like Facebook. They help broadcast our plight," said Lina.

"I agree. The military can tame the local media—but they can't control the foreign media," said Kuan Hee.

"I hope they won't get the ISPs to shut down access to Facebook," said Tim.

"I think it's only a matter of time," said Jordan.

CHAPTER 9

It was near the end of September. Kuan Hee's parents had been awaiting, albeit in vain, news of Kuan Hee's fate in the aftermath of the City Hall confrontation. They had received neither letters nor e-mails from the police or the military government. They were getting anxious. *Will he be charged for his role in the protest?* they wondered.

When Kuan Hee came down from his bedroom, his parents were in a pensive mood in the living room.

"We can't be calling the police to find out whether you will be charged," said his father.

"But, we can't keeping waiting," said his mother. "The suspense is killing me."

"I'm sorry for giving you guys so much trouble," said Kuan Hee.

"It's not you," said his mother. "You did nothing wrong."

"Yes, son. Your mother is right," said his father. "You did the right thing, fighting for our freedom."

"We are proud of you, dear," said his mother. "So proud."

"We thought you were getting too soft," said his father. "We were regretting we didn't give you the opportunity to voice your views—to speak your mind."

"What your father means to say is—we have been overprotective parents," said his mother. "Isn't that right, dear?"

"Of course, dear," said his father.

"It isn't that we didn't want brothers or sisters for you," said his mother. "We tried very hard—but—"

"It's not your mother's fault," said his father. "Nature hasn't been generous with us."

"Aw. It's OK, Mum and Dad," said Kuan Hee. "Serious. I am very happy. I have Mum and Dad; I have my friends, Lina and Tim. I'm satisfied."

"I'm sure you are, dear," said his mother.

"Can—can I remain in the union?" asked Kuan Hee.

"Dear, if you stay in the union, you are courting trouble," said his mother. "These are different times. We are under military rule."

"But, Mum and Dad, just now you were saying how good it was for me to be more vocal—more proactive," said Kuan Hee.

"Yes, I know," said his father. "Still—I feel uncomfortable about it."

"I'll be careful—I promise." said Kuan Hee. "Please, please."

"Let me think…" said his father.

"Dad, I want to be able to do something good—useful for the country," said Kuan Hee. "I promise I won't be rash."

"Alright—alright," said his father. "But—be careful OK?"

"Thanks Dad, and Mum," said Kuan Hee. "Thanks a million."

WHATSAPP:

"Meet at ToastBox 11:00 a.m.," texted Lina.

"Will be slightly late," texted Tim.

"K," texted Kuan Hee.
"Bring AleXander," texted Lina.
"K," texted Kuan Hee.

ToastBox on basement one of Hougang Mall was their other go-to watering hole. There was a smattering of customers at this modern-day take of the traditional coffee shop; it was not yet lunch time. Hunched over a table at a corner, Kuan Hee and Lina engaged in small talk while waiting for Tim.

"Is your mother still fuming over the incident?"

"She has forgotten about it—thank God for that."

"Will I be welcome at your place?"

"Of course you will. My mum doesn't keep grudges. Anyway, it's not you she's mad with; it's me."

"When—when I was shot, were you shocked?"

"You know the answer."

"I'm sorry." Kuan Hee put his hand over hers, and tightened its grip. Then he massaged it.

"It's OK. It's already over so long ago."

"I heard you wouldn't stop crying."

"Did you? Who told you?" Lina's voice was getting croaky.

"Someone—I heard you were trembling."

"In that situation, anyone would, you know."

"Thanks."

"For what?"

"For caring about me."

"Mmm."

"Can I hop over later?"

"If you want to."

"Your Mum?"

"I already told you she's alright now."

"*Wah*. Sitting side by side already," said Tim. "Hope I'm not disturbing you guys."

"Tim," said Kuan Hee. "Have you heard?"

"What?" said Tim.

"Jordan's the new man in charge of the union," said Kuan Hee.

"Won't that make his old man angry?" asked Tim.

"Tim says he doesn't care," said Kuan Hee.

"He doesn't mean it, Kuan Hee," said Tim. "He's his parents' pet, you know. I'm sure he's not that cruel."

"I have taken Jordan's place," said Kuan Hee.

"I expected it," said Tim. "But, I thought your parents are against the idea."

"They finally caved in to my request," said Kuan Hee.

"Great," said Tim. "I think they know the military won't be hard on us."

"Why do you say that?" asked Lina.

"I've been thinking," said Tim. "With Jordan by our side, his father will think twice before he does anything to hurt us. It's tantamount to hurting his own son."

"Yeah, Tim's right," said Lina.

"I don't quite agree," said Kuan Hee.

"Why?" said Tim.

"Well, Jordan was with us at City Hall, right?" said Kuan Hee. "And we suffered much damage."

"*Aiyoh*. Kuan Hee's right," said Lina.

"Just whose side are you on, Lina?" said Tim.

"Both arguments make sense," said Lina. "But—Kuan Hee's makes more sense."

"*Alamak*. Lina," said Tim. "You guys are one voice."

"We are not only one voice," retorted Lina. "We're also one couple."

"*Alamak*," said Tim. "I give up talking to you."

Kuan Hee took his two friends to a large field in Changi. What they saw in front of them was a bare flat piece of grassy land with no trees for as far as the eye could see. They put down their backpacks and sat on the grass.

"I didn't know that Singapore has got such a big field," said Lina.

"There are a few more—if we bother to look for them," said Kuan Hee. "These are all state land."

"What?" said Lina. "And we keep hearing people complain we are short of land in Singapore."

"Kuan Hee, take out the robots," said Tim. "Let's have a look at them."

"I only brought Alex," said Kuan Hee. "My father says not to bring out both at the same time."

"One or two, doesn't make any difference," said Tim.

"Alex. Alex, come out," said Kuan Hee.

"He can understand commands?" said Tim.

"Of course, he can," said Kuan Hee. The robot peeked out of the backpack. Then it lifted itself out of the bag and somersaulted onto the grass. It got to its feet and stood at attention. Alex was a handsome robot. It stood about thirty centimetres tall. It sported black hair and had glassy eyes. Its entire body was metallic silver in colour. You could see the joints on its arms, hips and knees. It was wearing a pair of boots. Lina and Tim were captivated by it, unable to utter a single word.

"Alex," said Kuan Hee. "Say hallo to Lina and Tim."

"Hi Lina. Hi Tim. Glad to meet you," said Alex the robot.

"Wah. I must say I'm impressed," said Tim. "It—I mean he is unlike any robot I have ever seen. He's agile."

"Yes, and fast too," said Lina.

"What's in this?" said Tim, pointing to a rectangular outline on the torso of the robot.

"Don't know," said Kuan Hee. "I asked my father. He said he would let me in on the secret compartment soon."

"Wow. A secret compartment," said Tim. "Bet you it conceals some weapons."

"Don't be silly, Tim. It's so small," said Lina.

"Lina, aren't you also studying nano-technology?" said Tim. Lina blushed.

"What is the robot made of?" said Lina.

"My father says it's gold-titanium alloy—four times

stronger than titanium," said Kuan Hee.

"It must be expensive. It's gold you know," said Lina.

"Is it indestructible?" said Tim.

"It's been coated with a special liquid chemical—state of the art material. It's like armor," said Kuan Hee. "My father says the liquid looks like custard. But, it's strong stuff."

"Custard?" said Lina. "But, it's—it's so squishy."

"Can I test it?" said Tim.

"How?" said Kuan Hee.

"By throwing it a distance," said Tim.

"Aw. Don't be naughty," said Lina.

"Go ahead, Tim," said Kuan Hee. "I'm sure Alex won't mind."

"Of course, he won't, Kuan Hee," said Lina. "He's a robot, for goodness's sake. Robots have got no feelings. They also can't think."

"Not this one, Lina—not this one," said Kuan Hee.

"You mean, Alex can decide if he wants us to throw him?" said Lina,

"Alex," said Kuan Hee. "Can I throw you over a distance?"

"If you wish to, yes, of course," said Alex the robot.

"*Wah*. He sure is intelligent," said Lina. She was impressed.

"May I, Alex?" said Tim.

"Yes, please," said Alex the robot. Gripping the robot, Tim placed it under his jawbone and flung the robot as if he was throwing a shot put. The robot flew in a trajectory over the open space and landed on the grass about thirty feet away.

As quickly as it landed, the robot jumped to its feet and strode across the field back to where the three were. Then it stood at attention.

"Gosh. There's no dent on it," said Tim. It looks brand new."

"Don't believe me right?" said Kuan Hee.

"Alex runs pretty fast," said Lina. "When does its battery run out?"

"He runs on solar power," said Kuan Hee. "The whole surface of the robot is embedded with tiny solar panels."

"Wah. I didn't know they could make solar panels so small that I can't even see them," said Tim. "Unbelievable. I sure have a lot to learn about nano technology."

"Does it sleep?" said Lina.

"No, it doesn't, Lina," said Kuan Hee. "But, it does need to recharge—every week," said Kuan Hee. "That's why Alex is here—He's taking in sunlight energy."

"How do you know it's fully recharged?" said Lina.

"Boy, you sure do have a lot of questions," said Kuan Hee. "I don't have all the answers, though. Let me ask my father when I get home."

The foursome had a pretty good time together that day. Little Alex entertained the others with his little antics, while the three pals marveled at his ability to engage them in conversation.

CHAPTER 10

It was a wet Christmas; it was pouring with rain every other day. Kuan Hee and the two robots were getting along nicely. The past few months of friendship between them had endeared the robots to Kuan Hee. He wasn't lonely at home anymore; they had become his pals. In his bedroom, the robots stood side by side, eyes wide open, and hands clasped, on a desk next to the window. They could now compete with Lina for his attention. She wasn't pleased when Kuan Hee refused to meet her a couple of times on the pretext of having loads of homework to complete. He was actually playing with Alex and Xander, getting to know them and their capabilities better.

Kuan Hee's father had revealed the secret behind the square panel on the front of the robots. Alex and Xander had lethal weapons hidden in them. His father had held Alex in one hand and pressed a protruding button on the back of the robot. The front panel had swung open exposing what looked like a mishmash of tiny gear mechanisms and armatures. In its centre was a round plate with shafts fanning out of a protruding lens. His father had said this little contraption was a laser weapon system capable of producing fifty thousand watts of energy. It could burn through virtually anything within thirty metres.

Xander's front panel, when open, revealed three small rockets on launchers standing parallel to the robot's body. At the elder Wang's command, the rockets leaned at an angle to the panel. His father had said this was a miniature version of rocket artillery used by the army. There was no recoil, unlike gun artillery, so little Xander would not be knocked onto the ground each time a rocket was fired. A single rocket could blast through an army tank—it was that deadly.

Kuan Hee was mesmerized by the gadgetry. His father was indeed a genius. He remembered his father had also warned him against playing with the deadly weapons. He could only use them when facing a life-or-death situation.

The robots' weapons, his father had explained, could only be activated if the front panel was open. When shut, the robots could not fire the weapons on their own. It was a safety measure, according to his father. While he felt Alex and Xander were kind robots who could be counted on to do good only, he was also worried they might make a wrong decision on their own. So, he had included a manually operated door in the otherwise futuristic robot. It was a precaution he had to incorporate in the robot's design.

It was at this time that Lina was getting jealous of—of all things—Alex and Xander. To her, the Christmas season was a time to be spent with loved ones, doing window shopping sprees and huddling together in the cold wet weather. But, it was not to be, for Kuan Hee was instead spending more time with his two 'toys'. However, to Kuan Hee, these were not mere toys; these were intelligent robots with a propensity to think. Why, he had even put aside his favourite online games to make more time to play with his robots.

Thus began a spate of petty quarrels between Lina and Kuan Hee over the strange three-sided relationship: Lina, Kuan Hee and his robots. When they finally met, Lina would scowl at him and give him the cold shoulder on a cold day when they should have been cuddling each other instead.

It was a difficult time for Kuan Hee with Lina blowing hot and cold every other day. Now, they couldn't decide on simple matters such as where to meet or what place to eat at. It was getting frustrating. Kuan Hee would sometimes ask her whether her *ta yi ma* had arrived for a visit. It was a euphemism for her having her period. Indeed, she would admit to having her period but pour cold water over the connection between her behaviour and the menstruation period. Altogether, it wasn't a merry Christmas for the couple.

Things got to a boil one afternoon when Kuan Hee missed their appointment at NEX Shopping Mall. They had agreed to meet outside a bank in the atrium of the mall. He had stood her up. He had plain forgotten. And in their WhatsApp conversation, she had vowed not to leave the spot until Kuan Hee appeared. He had to put away his two robots and scrambled off to meet her.

In her home, everyone—her mother and her three brothers—gave in to her. She was the youngest, and the only girl in the family, so they would pander to her whimsical needs. It was, therefore, conceivable that she would expect the same of Kuan Hee.

"Sorry, sorry—I'm late," said Kuan Hee. "A thousand apologies."

"You're not late," said Lina. "You are very late."

"I was busy doing my homework," said Kuan Hee. "I forgot the time."

"Even my brothers don't dare do this to me," said Lina.

"Sorry," said Kuan Hee. "I promise I won't do it again." He was used to her princess-like behavior and knew it was futile to talk back to her when she was in one of these 'strange' moods. Meek obedience was the only thing that would assuage her anger. To him, being late was a small matter; she was making a mountain out of a molehill. But, that was her trademark. And early in their friendship she had registered this trademark with him. So he knew she would not fail to use it.

"I'll tell my mother what you did to me," said Lina. Tears were welling in her eyes. She was sniffling. But, they were in the middle of crowd. He could not have her crying in front of so many eyes. It would be embarrassing.

Kuan Hee brought her to watch a movie. He whispered sweet nothings into her ears in the cinema. He took her to eat her favourite Hazelnuts and Chocolate ice cream at Anderson's. *Oh, the things I have to do to pacify her*, he lamented.

"Kuan Hee," said Lina. "I want…I want."

They had come out of Hougang MRT Station and were walking towards her block of flats. Of course he knew what she wanted. How could he not know? She had been dropping a hint here and there the past few weeks. First, little ones, then direct hints. Any fool could not mistake the message she was sending him.

Being of reticent character, he was slow to react to her moves. It wasn't that he did not love her. There wasn't any other girl in his life, for God's sake. It was simply he was reluctant to make the first move—and for no rhyme or reason. They were both of marriageable age. There wasn't anything standing in their way—except for Alex and Xander the robots, of course.

Is today to be a moment of great love for us? he wondered.

"Kuan Hee," said Lina. "Are you listening? Are you paying attention?" She was getting cross. Was she about to exercise her trademark again? Then she leaned against Kuan Hee. Their pace was getting slower. Her weight on him was making their walk tedious.

Kuan Hee didn't realize it then, but, he had made a right turn towards Jalan Naung, instead of treading a straight path on to her home.

The couple found themselves in Kuan Hee's bedroom.

His parents were not home; he had just found out. They had the whole house to themselves.

Is she getting a little horny? he wondered. *Am I getting excited?* he wondered again. His heart was pounding in his thumb. He could feel its reverberation in the twitching of his thumb.

Then came that moment—their moment of great love.

"The condom—I don't have it."

"I don't want—no sensation."

"You want me on top?"

"Yes."

"My hands—can touch?"

"Yes."

"Can bite?"

"Nibble, *lah*—bite—painful *lah*."

"Your hips, so big; I didn't realize."

"My mother says…big hips—more children."

"Mmmm."

"So strong, yours."

"Then?"

"Ouch!"

"Oh."

"Painful, you know."

"Sorry."

"That's better."

"Can go in?"

"Wait a while. We girls need more sensation, you know."

"Can go in now?"

"A little longer."

"Suckle me."

"Mmm."

"More—more."

"Mmmm."

"Can go in now?"

"Yessss—"

"Cannot go in leh. Hole too small. So tight, painful."

"Me painful too."

"Feel anything?"

"A tingling sensation. Faster—faster—"

"Still a little tight. I'm using all my strength."

"Faster. Use more force."

"I am going as fast as I can."

"Deeper—deeper–"

"I'm trying—really—"

"What's the smell? What's that liquid?"

"Lubrication—natural lubrication."

"So much? It's gooey—like nail polish remover."

"Aw…Faster."

"Coming out!"

"What?"

"Don't touch…wait…wait. It's sensitive."

"OK."

"Not sensitive now. Going in again."

"You know I've been waiting for you, don't you."

"Mmm."

"Faster, please."

"Mmm."

"Coming out—I can't stop it. Oops!—it's all over your belly button. And—"

"It's all over me—my breasts too. So much sperm. You're so strong—Gee! It's warm and sticky—squishy like raw egg white."

"Let me clean it up. I'll get some tissue paper."

"Ouch. My leg. You just pressed your leg on my leg."

"Sorry."

"I'll wipe your big brother—no, it's little brother now. It's getting spongy. And droopy."

"Mmm."

"It's alive again. It's pushing against my fingers; it's growing in my hand…I—I want more."

"But I'm tired."

"More—more—"

"Next time, can? No more strength…need a break."

"Aw. You're bad. I hate you."

Lina snuggled up against Kuan Hee's warm chest, planting small little kisses on it. *Tomorrow, perhaps,* she thought. He ruffled her long hair and gave it little pecks.

"I love you, Kuan Hee—I really do."

"Me too. Love you…lots."

"Why didn't you…why didn't we…"

"I—I."

"Ouch!" Lina had given him a love bite on his neck.

"That's to remember today."

"Mmm."

"I—I don't want to get pregnant…I'm only twenty-one."

"I know."

"I'm a little afraid…getting pregnant."

"I know."

It was the first time for both of them. It was awkward for both. But, it was pleasurable for both. Lina wrapped her arms around Kuan Hee and closed her eyes. Her head was now resting on his arm. It was awkward for Kuan Hee; his arm was getting numb, but he couldn't move it; he didn't want to wake her. She stirred in her sleep. Both had become intimate. Before, they were bosom friends; now they were a couple. He didn't want to interrupt her sweet dreams. Soon it was morning.

"You forgot to call home," said Kuan Hee.

"Nope, I did not," said Lina. "I told my mum I was spending the night with a girlfriend, mugging for a test."

"What if Tim finds out—about us?" asked Kuan Hee.

"Mmm?" said Lina.

CHAPTER 11

It was a year after the military takeover. The citizenry was cowed by the relentless efforts of the National Reconciliation Council to control dissent in the country. Singapore had become a police state. The press and the broadcast stations had become a parrot for the military government's propaganda. Social media were being monitored around the clock by the army's Cyber Watch Group, whose original function was to prevent cyber attacks by foreign elements. Its actions were pervasive. The Group had a few thousand personnel working round the clock, filtering posts and comments on local and foreign social media.

Local media were served with shutdown notices whenever anti-government articles or comments were found on their Websites. It was more difficult to control foreign social media such as Facebook so the government blocked locals' access to these Websites. However, it was easy to circumvent the orders. People flocked to foreign Websites providing Virtual Private Networks.

Telecom companies too had a hard time, for the army stationed personnel at their exchanges to listen in to the telephone conversations of individuals deemed to be subversives. All data routed through the telecom networks were routinely filtered by the army's CWG.

The government was trying to create an atmosphere of mistrust among its citizens. People were enticed with privileges and benefits each time they reported misdeeds of their friends, acquaintances or neighbours who were arrested on trumped-up charges.

In spite of the concerted efforts of the government, residents' camaraderie remained high. People found ways to work around the inconveniences brought about by the government. The presence of foreign social media on the Internet, no doubt, spurred their never-say-die spirits. Netizens from all over the world continued to type messages of support for the people of Singapore. Some composed inspirational songs cajoling Singaporeans to stand up for their country.

Thus, the circumstances gave birth to a new underground movement named SAVE SG. People from all walks of life embraced SAVE SG's noble aims. They used social media to get their messages across to fellow residents. It was easy as frequenting these Websites had become second nature to locals here. People had become helpless without social media, for a way of life had been woven around such media.

University students led by Temasek University's student union hosted a commemoration of the first anniversary of the army's brutal crackdown on protesters outside City Hall. Jordan was to take the stage to deliver a belated eulogy to honour the late Donald Chen and lament the death of democracy in Singapore. But he went missing on the day of the event. So Kuan Hee had to hastily prepare a speech for the occasion.

The plan was to march as a peaceful procession from Cavenagh Bridge to St Andrew's Road, retracing the route of student protesters on the day of the army crackdown at City Hall. But the army had got wind of the event. Metal barricades had been put up to block both sides of St

Andrew's Road, and armored personnel carriers stood at the entrances to the road.

Kuan Hee and fellow student leaders from the other local universities then decided to stage a protest march along Orchard Road—where tourists flocked. Groups from several civic organisations had indicated their wish to participate in the event. So, SAVE SG PROTEST MARCH was born. It now had a critical mass.

Thousands of protesters, from the universities and their alumni associations to professional and civic groups, moved through Orchard Road, watched by thousands from all walks of life, including curious tourists.

The military government had stationed several companies of soldiers along both sides of the route. There were armored personnel carriers and water cannons at the junctions. It had failed to stop the protest, but it was determined not to let the protesters run riot in the streets, not in Singapore.

It was Kuan Hee's first major test as a leader of men; he had been a squad leader in his national service days, but that didn't count. He performed admirably well, and received praises from others. The one most impressed, of course, was his other half—Lina.

Today, the army was restrained in its behavior. It could be due to the presence of picture-snapping tourists or the watching eyes of the foreign press who were reporting on the event for their country's consumption. So, the event went without a hitch. After today, SAVE SG became internationally known.

Jordan remained unreachable for the next few days. Kuan Hee's calls to his smartphone went unanswered. Jordan's friends could not contact him too. They were unable to visit his residence as the street where his house stood had been cordoned off. Soldiers guarded both ends of the street. No one could enter it without an invitation from the army. His house was now the official residence of the Supreme Leader of the NRC.

One evening, as Kuan Hee was watching television in his bedroom, he heard a noise at the balcony. Someone or some creature was making a noise there. He grabbed the nearest thing he could use as a weapon and pushed aside the glass door. It was Jordan! He had scaled the pipes on the outside wall of the house. Jordan was wearing his trademark cap. He looked tense and Kuan Hee could hear his heavy breathing in the quiet of the surroundings.

"Where have you been?"

"Can we go inside?"

"Here—take a seat."

"Kuan Hee, come away from the window. Do you have something to eat?"

"I can rustle up something. How about Maggie mee?"

"That will be great."

"Come downstairs with me."

"Are your parents home?"

"Nope. They are out attending a dinner function."

"OIC."

"Some vegetables for you?"

"Sure. Let me help with the bowls." Soon they were seated in the dining room. Jordan slurped up the noodles. It was as if he had not eaten in days. Kuan Hee resisted the urge to ask more questions. He didn't want Jordan to choke on the food.

They were not close friends and, as far as he knew, Jordan did not know where he was living. Kuan Hee found it strange that Jordan had turned up at his place.

Kuan Hee repeated his question. "Where have you been?"

"My father kept me locked up in the house. He wouldn't let me go out, no matter what I said."

"He didn't want you to attend the protest?"

"It's not just that. Do you have a drink?" Kuan Hee opened the fridge and retrieved a Coke for Jordan.

Jordan placed his NY cap on the table. Kuan Hee could now have a better look at his face. His eyes sported dark rings. He didn't appear to have slept well.

"Can you put me up here?"

Ordinarily, if it was Tim, Kuan Hee would not have spared a second thought. But, this was Jordan. His father was the military ruler of Singapore. There would be repercussions if he let him stay over, especially since he had left home without his father's knowledge.

"It would be difficult, you know—your Dad is a bigshot. He might not like the idea."

"Kuan Hee, help me, please." Jordan was now pleading with him. He still hadn't disclosed the real reason. *Should I let him stay, or shouldn't I?* thought Kuan Hee. He was in two minds. Lina was not here, otherwise he would have asked her for her opinion. Finally, he relented.

His parents came home past midnight and retired to their bedroom promptly. His mother did not pop into his bedroom. The two men shared Kuan Hee's bed. It was king-sized and both weren't big-sized. On the bed, Kuan Hee recounted the happenings during the protest in Orchard Road. Jordan steadfastly refused to divulge his reasons for leaving home; and Kuan Hee, ever the good host, did not press on with his questioning.

However, Jordan did talk about his father. He rambled about his father's unhappiness with the previous government. They had overlooked him for promotion to General. A young President's scholar in the elite administrative service had the honour of becoming the first Brigadier-General to lead the FF Brigade. Colonel Tee was relegated to second in command when the young upstart took over the reins. Then he nursed his grievances with the administration. They didn't recognise talent, he had said to his son. They would rather promote untested individuals who lacked experience. The only thing they had was an honours degree in some ivy-league university in the United States. What did they know about running an army?, he would complain to his son. These were mere boy scouts, wet behind their ears—he would blare into his son's ears.

Then he would boast about how he got into the good books of the deceased Prime Minister, doing everything that he hated so that the PM would trust him and let him run important departments in government. It was a god-send, he would tell his son. He managed to wrestle control of essential services in the armed forces, though he was, in his own words, 'a mere colonel'. That's when he hatched the plot to take over the government. He felt he had to put things right—make sure deserving people in the service would be promoted, regardless of their education level. That was why his trusted lieutenants were now running the country with him. To him, they were extraordinarily talented; to him they deserved the positions that he had given them now—heading the various important departments in the military government.

Kuan Hee was all ears—Jordan was telling him things that no one else in government or Singapore had privy knowledge of.

The plainclothes came looking for Jordan the next day. They admitted they had no search warrant, but they didn't need them, in this day and age, to run their dirty fingers over every nook and crevice in the house.

Earlier, hearing vehicles stopping outside the gate, Kuan Hee had hidden Jordan in the secret cellar. He had hesitated before doing so, fearing his father's secret might be leaked out. But, the exigency of the situation demanded urgent action—he made the urgent decision alone.

Kuan Hee didn't have time to hide Alex and Xander. The men had come too suddenly; he didn't have time to think. The two robots stood cheery-eyed throughout the search. The plainclothes apparently were too busy looking for a person to cast their eyes on things in the house. They left after a fruitless hunt.

WHATSAPP:
"Meet at Kovan MRT @ 11:00 a.m.,"
texted Kuan Hee.
"Why?" texted Lina.
"Bringing J out," texted Kuan Hee.
"Jordan?" texted Lina.
"Yeah," texted Kuan Hee.
"How about Tim?" texted Lina.
"Not this time," texted Kuan Hee.

Kuan Hee wanted to keep Jordan's name out of the chat; he was afraid the government would be monitoring online conversations. But, it was too late. Lina had blurted out his name. Anyway, it was just possible they would miss this conversation; after all there were many thousands of conversations being carried out every minute in Singapore. How could the government keep track of everything? But, he was wrong, of course. The government had access to supercomputers that could crunch big data to make sense of the information in no time.

The trio were careful not to let Jordan use his bank cards or MRT cards for the day's transactions. They were afraid such transactions would pinpoint Jordan's location. Jordan had left home prepared with some money from his piggy bank.

From Orchard MRT Station, they walked to Wisma Atria and Takashimaya, enjoying the strong air-conditioning—a proper respite from the hot weather outside. At 313 Orchard, the guys browsed the New Era store where Jordan eagerly fingered the latest caps on display on the wall. He chose a black NY cap and paid for it with cash. All three had a jolly good time that afternoon.

They were in Somerset MRT Station when Jordan spotted some men milling around the 7-Eleven Store. His face turned pale. He tapped on Kuan Hee's shoulder, gesturing that they reverse tracks and leave the station. Alas, it was too late. The eagle-eyed men had seen him.

They made quick steps towards the three. Kuan Hee grabbed Lina's hand and together, they made a dash for 313 Orchard with the men in hot pursuit.

They ran through 313 Orchard, passed Orchard Gateway and were about to cross the underground passageway to CentrePoint Shopping Centre when they stopped in their tracks. In front of them, at the other end of the passageway, were some burly plainclothes. They were trapped. The plainclothes approached them. They caught hold of Jordan and hurried him off, leaving Kuan Hee and Lina bewildered. Clearly, these guys were not interested in them.

"How did the plainclothes manage to find us?" Kuan Hee said to Lina. She did not know the answer either.

"Was it the WhatsApp chat that led them to us?"

"If it was so, then they would have caught us at Kovan."

"Yeah—just how did they do it?"

The duo were momentarily lost. The men had taken the group by surprise, and they had yet to recover from the shock. They walked in CentrePoint Shopping Centre directionless.

Then they decided to head home. As they walked through the gate into Somerset MRT Station, Kuan Hee looked at the monitor screens overhead. It showed a live video of them moving through the gate. It dawned on him that the cameras in the MRT stations had captured them going in and out of the stations. *Our movements are being recorded,* he said to himself.

"It's the cameras—they gave our position away."

"How can they? There must be more than a hundred stations on the island with a few thousand cameras altogether. How can they monitor all the cameras? They will need many, many men."

"Nope, you are wrong, Lina—they use facial recognition software. They use supercomputers which can process tremendous amounts of data received from the cameras—makes sense, alright."

"That's bad, real bad—there's no way we can hide from these cameras—unless we don't use the MRT or the bus."

"Yeah. It's bad news alright."

CHAPTER 12

Lina followed Kuan Hee back to Jalan Naung. Both were spending an inordinate amount of time alone at his house. They were now intimate, having moved on to more love-making trysts since their very first experience in his bedroom. Kuan Hee's mother was waiting in the living room. Her lips were pursed; she was a bundle of nerves. Apparently, something had upset her.

"Kuan Hee. Kuan Hee—your father's missing," she said.

"Not again, Mum," said Kuan Hee. "He didn't call you the whole day?"

"Not since this morning," said his mother. "He never misses the lunch time call."

His mother was right. In their forty-two years of marriage, he had never missed a single lunch time call, except the time when the army shut down his workplace when they usurped power.

"Mum, you know Dad—he could have forgotten the time. You know when he's at work, nothing else matters," said Kuan Hee.

"But, he's never like this, not in a million years."

Kuan Hee and Lina retreated into their private space,

leaving his mother to her thoughts. *Come morning, he will be home*, thought Kuan Hee as he snuggled into bed with his beloved.

But, morning came and went. There was still no sign of Kuan Hee's father. By nightfall, his mother was expecting the worst. *He had to be in detention*, she thought. But, there was no way to get hold of him. Her calls to his office-cum-laboratory went unanswered. The receptionist said he hadn't come in the last two days. *She is lying*, thought his mother. *Lying through her teeth! That's what it is.*

Kuan Hee could call his father with the implanted mobile device, but he had forgotten about it. Then the moment came. There was a voice in his brain. It was calling out to him. *Am I dreaming?* he wondered. There went the voice again. It sounded like his father; in fact, it was his father. He was sure this time.

Son, son, can you hear me? the voice in his mind said.

Was his father talking to him in his dreams? But, he wasn't dreaming. It was broad daylight and he was alone in his bedroom. Then it hit him. He realized his father had been calling him on the implanted phone in his arm. He had plain forgotten about the device.

"Kuan Hee, please answer me," said his father's voice.

"Now, how do I talk to Father?" Kuan Hee asked aloud. He remembered the notes he had written about his father's strange contraptions. He retrieved the note from a drawer in his desk. He flipped the pages. *Here it is,* he told himself.

> To call, say **LOGON ALPHA** aloud.
> To talk to the other party, speak aloud.
> To end call, say **TEN FOUR ALPHA**

"LOGON ALPHA."

"Kuan Hee, It's me, Dad. Can you hear me?"

"Dad, I can hear you. Are you alright? Mum's worried sick about you. You didn't call home the past few days." It was information overload. Kuan Hee had rattled the string of sentences without a pause. It was too much for his father's brain to process. The electrical impulses took time to convert to signals that his brain would understand.

"Kuan Hee—slow down, slow down, please."

"S-o-r-r-y D-a-D."

"No need to be that slow, son."

"Sorry."

"I was saying—Mum misses you."

"I miss her too, please tell her that for me."

"Dad, where are you?"

"I have been held against my will, son."

"Who? Why?"

"Colonel Tee's men, son."

"Why, Dad?"

"They want me to carry out a secret operation for them. I refused, so they are keeping me hostage till I agree."

"What? Secret operation? What's that, Dad?"

"It's a long story, son. In a nutshell, they want me to transfer someone's memories into another person's."

"Who's this person, Dad?"

"Colonel Tee, son."

"The dictator?"

"Yes, son."

"Will they harm you, Dad, if you go against their wishes?"

"I don't think so—not for now anyway. They need me. I'm important to them. But, they may harm people dear to me—to make me do what they want."

"They want to harm Mum?"

"Yes, son—and you, too."

"Can't we run away?"

"I can't, but you and your mother can. I want you two to get out of the country—this instant."

"Dad, Mum won't do it. She'll never leave you, you know that."

"Son, you must try to persuade her. Talk to her now. Pack the essentials and leave immediately. Go out of harm's way. If they can't find you, they can't change my mind. But they know you are my Achilles' heel."

"I will, Dad. How do I get in touch with you? Where are they holding you?"

"Use the implant, son. You can call me using the implanted phone. If I don't answer—just keep trying. And, I'm in a lab somewhere—not sure where. It's not at my workplace definitely."

"OK. Dad."

"Don't use the SIM card in your iPhone. Use the Polaris SIM—it's in the cellar—top shelf—in a box. It's linked to a satellite."

The connection was broken. His father had terminated the call.

"Dad? Hallo Dad. Dad?" *He's gone offline,* Kuan Hee told himself. *Got to tell Mum.*

Try as he might, he could not persuade his mother to leave the country—not without his father. When she had cooled down from knocking down the idea, she took to chiding him for implanting the mobile device in his arm. Then she stopped her racket. It was the mobile device that had come to their aid during these difficult times. Without it, the family would have been hopelessly pining for his father. The device was indeed a good idea. It had taken a brilliant chap to come up with such a magical piece of work, his mother told him. It took someone with foresight to have seen this situation coming, his mother added. Then she cried again. His mother was missing his father again. He went bleary eyed whenever he saw her crying.

I have got to change the SIM card, he told himself.

Kuan Hee retrieved the Polaris SIM card from the cellar and replaced the one in his iPhone with it. He turned on the iPhone. It was working. On the top left of the screen appeared the carrier's name: POLARIS.

The next day, Kuan Hee's mother went missing. She had gone marketing as she usually did at 6:00 a.m. It was already 9:45 a.m. And she was not home yet.

Kuan Hee went looking for her at the neighbourhood market where she usually shopped. Then Lina joined him. They walked around the neighbourhood, but there was no sign of his mother. She had vanished into thin air. He called his mother's friends, but they too had not seen her. Kuan Hee suddenly had a dreadful thought—she had been captured by Colonel Tee's men. *It has to be so,* he reasoned to himself. He had to call his father.

Back at Jalan Naung, with Lina seated beside him, he phoned his father. There was no reply. He tried again. Still no answer. *Is Father asleep?* Kuan Hee wondered. *It's almost lunch time; he couldn't be sleeping in the middle of the day. Is someone with him? That's a possibility.* He decided to try again in half an hour. Soon, the suspense was getting to his nerves. He paced up and down his bedroom. He didn't notice—Lina's eyes were welling.

"LOGON ALPHA."

"Dad, are you there?" There was silence in his mind.

"Hallo Dad. Hallo." He couldn't hear anything in his mind.

Lina was choking back her tears. She too was anxious. "Can you leave a message?"

"It doesn't have an Inbox. Everything is done on the fly."

"Keep trying."

"Dad. Calling Dad. Answer me, Dad."

"Son, I am here. I'm listening."

"Dad. They have taken Mum."

"I know son. Colonel Tee was here just now."

"Dad, what should I do?"

"Keep safe, son. Go into hiding. They may come looking for you."

"But, where can I hide?"

"Go stay with a friend—stay with Tim. And bring AleXander and the flies with you."

"Is Mum alright?"

"They have not let me see your Mum yet. Maybe—today they will."

"I'm sorry, Dad. I should have watched Mum carefully."

"Isn't your fault, son. Isn't your fault." Then there was a hollow sound in his mind; his father had gone offline.

"My father wants me to hide at Tim's place."

"Can't you hide in the secret cellar?"

"They will be watching the gate."

"You can climb the—"

"I can't take the risk. I'm the only one left—Dad and Mum have been caught. I can't let them catch me."

"How about staying with me?"

"Your house? But, it's too crowded. There are five of you in there."

"You and I can occupy one room, my mother and oldest brother one, and my two other brothers one—just nice." Lina's face lit up. She wasn't teary anymore.

"Does your mother mind? Will your brothers mind?"

"Don't worry. I call the shots in the house."

"I may get them into trouble, you know."

"But—we are one big family—you, me and my family."

CHAPTER 13

Lina and her family lived in a four-roomed HDB flat in Hougang Avenue Five. It was lively in her home; there wasn't a moment of silence in the flat, not with three grown-up brothers and her mother all bumping into one another as they went about doing their things in the small space. Kuan Hee was unaccustomed to living in small spaces. His semi-detached home—all two floors of it—housed his father, mother and him. There were three bedrooms upstairs and one downstairs—more than enough for them.

At 79 Jalan Naung, Kuan Hee had the whole bathroom to himself. Here, he had to queue up to use the bathroom. But Lina tried her best to make him feel at home. She told her mother to share the second bedroom with her eldest brother. She herself would occupy the master bedroom with Kuan Hee. It had its own adjoining bathroom, but no water heater though—that was in the common bathroom in the kitchen. *Kuan Hee will be pleased—no need to use the common bathroom,* she thought.

Lina's mother never asked why she was living together with a man. She didn't have to explain to her brother that the couple were merely sharing the room—not cohabiting.

They had seen Lina and Kuan Hee going out with each other since she was in primary school. It was only natural that they would eventually marry each other—so there wasn't any need to bother about the requirement to get married first before they could *tong fang*. It was already the 2030s—no need to follow traditional Chinese values to the letter. And her eldest brother had told Kuan Hee to take good care of his little sister.

Theirs was a typical *Hokkien* family, where the household revolved around the matriarch—her mother; only that in Lina's home, the matriarch's authority had been supplanted by little *Huang Ah Ma*—Lina! Like all other arrangements in the household, the Goh family was accepting of this one. After all, Lina ruled the house.

At dinner time, her brothers would gesture to Kuan Hee, and ask him to eat, to eat more. Her mother would keep the chicken drumstick for him. That was their way of making him feel welcome. Soon he settled down at Block 308.

But the police cameras in the void deck—keeping watch of the two lift lobbies and staircases in the block bothered Kuan Hee. He was sure these cameras were connected to some central monitoring authority—the military government could track his movements easily. Using facial recognition technology, they could find him effortlessly. He should not continue staying here; he would be putting the Goh family in trouble if the plainclothes came for him. In the meantime, whenever he went out of the flat, he would wear a baseball cap and cover his face with a flyer.

But now, I have to find out more about Colonel Tee, Kuan Hee thought. *Yes, I've got to spy on his house.*

Jordan had told Kuan Hee where he lived. In fact, Jordan had said many more things about his parents. The Tee family lived in Belmont Road, off Holland Road, in the upscale Holland area. The house had belonged to

Jordan's maternal grandfather. Upon his grandfather's death, his mother had inherited the property. Colonel Tee had an inferiority complex. He thought his wife was too good for him. He had felt insecure when he was dating her, and her father didn't make things easier on him. Her father was always harping on his inability to provide a good life for her—his only child. When they married, Colonel Tee was only a lowly Lieutenant in the Rangers. Instead of getting their own house, they lived with her father in the Belmont Road bungalow. He had to put up with his father-in-law's idiosyncrasies. Colonel Tee vowed to make good one day. Indeed, he had done so, albeit in an evil way.

It had become standard practice for Kuan Hee to take AleXander and the two flies with him wherever he went. They sat comfortably in his spacious Crumpler backpack. Kuan Hee and Lina alighted from a taxi on busy Holland Road, next to a condominium. They made their way up a small road which forked into Belmont Road and Cornwall Gardens. Belmont Road had been cordoned off, but not Cornwall Gardens. The Tee bungalow nestled between the two roads.

Kuan Hee and Lina took up position on Cornwall Gardens. They brought out drawing blocks and some pencils. They were pretending to be young artists penciling the houses and trees there. She was wearing a straw hat and he a baseball cap—as disguise. Squatting on one side of the road, they didn't seem to blend into the area, try as they might. But they were a young couple whom nobody might take notice of. Ahead of the pair, up the slope on their side of the small road was a tennis court in the Tee residence. *This house is ultra big,* Lina thought. *Yes, opulent.*

Hardly any vehicles passed them this morning. Kuan Hee set the titanium housefly on his lap and let it take off into the air above them. In the silent surroundings, the housefly did not make any buzzing sound. Its wings took it over the tennis court into the swimming pool area where it danced and darted in rhythmic waves. The pair watched the small screen on the remote-control card intently.

"Moving nearer to the house. Looks like a two-storey bungalow."

"Fly into that window on the right, Kuan Hee."

"It's a sitting room. Nobody here. Let's turn right."

"It's got one, two, three—three bedrooms upstairs, like yours."

"Yeah, but slightly bigger. No one in here too. Not here also. The last one—the door's closed. Mmm. How about under the door? No good either. There are bristles on the bottom of the door—to keep cool air in."

"Can't see inside?"

"Let me use the infra-red scanner on its nose. Nope, the room's empty too."

"Mr Fly can sense heat?"

"Mr Fly can also smell—then it feeds the data into a decoder which identifies the smell."

"Wow!"

"Shush!"

"Kuan Hee, they can't hear us."

"Oh, I forgot, sorry."

"Don't go knocking into the furniture."

"Don't worry." He had had many dry runs with the two flies at home in the past few months. He had become proficient. *I've earned my flying licence,* he told himself.

Lina tapped his knee. "Wait." They took their eyes off the screen and pretended to be taking a perspective of the house across the road. A car was droning past them.

"Let's go downstairs."

The housefly flitted down the winding staircase with its elaborate balustrades. The pair admired the timber floorboards and columns which supported the bedrooms above. There seemed to be no one at home. Outside the house were some guards idling around in the compound.

Having been brought up in an HDB environment her whole life, Lina was not privy to how the rich in Singapore lived. Today was indeed an eye-opener for her. She had marveled at the size of Kuan Hee's semi-detached. But, this house was far bigger. *I didn't know Singapore has such big houses and gardens,* she told herself. *There must be at least a dozen big trees in the garden.*

"Let's call it a day. Let's come back another time."

"OK." The visit had not yielded any fruit. "We'll come back in the evening."

"Ha? So soon?"

"Jiving, just jiving. Tomorrow *lah.*"

"We've been busy today. By the way, have you named these drones yet?"

"Lina, these aren't drones—they're nano-robots."

"What shall we call them?"

"You just gave me an idea—your remark—'busy'. Shall we name them Busy and Tizzy?"

"Great. But who's who?"

"You say *lor.*"

"Housefly—Busy, and dragonfly—Tizzy."

"OK. Set."

"Let's go home, Busy and Tizzy."

CHAPTER 14

In the car park behind Block 308, there was an unmarked government car. Kuan Hee had learnt to recognize them by their QX prefix. He had seen such cars zip into SAFTI when he was doing guard duty during NS. *Are G men looking for me?* he wondered. He gestured to Lina for her to wait in the void deck of the opposite block, behind a pillar.

About half an hour later, they saw two men approaching the car. They had come out of Lina's block. Lina recognized one of them.

"It's a neighbour from upstairs. He has lived here for many years."

"OIC. Just being careful, Lina. Just being careful."

"You're being paranoic. That's what you are."

"You never know. We can all get into deep trouble—if they are Colonel Tee's men."

In Lina's bedroom, Kuan Hee let out his desire to move back into his house.

"But, they are looking for you. They'll be watching your house."

"There's this popular saying—the most dangerous place is the safest place."

"Please, *lah*. It's only a saying. What if they caught

you?"

"They won't. I'll be careful—very careful."

"Then I want to come along."

"But, it won't be convenient. And it's dangerous."

"I don't care. Either I tag along OR no deal."

Poor Kuan Hee, Lina was acting up again—like a princess. "Alright. Alright. But, does your mother mind?"

"She already knows we are together. She knows we go everywhere together. Besides, I am already twenty-one."

"OK. I get it. Pack some things and let's get going when darkness falls."

79 Jalan Nuang stood back to back with 85 Jalan Payoh Lai. The pair stole into the narrow passageway between the two semi-detached houses. Then Kuan Hee lifted Lina over the wall and soon they were tiptoeing along the cobbled backyard. It was dark, for the spotlights, usually controlled by a timer, were unlit.

Kuan Hee unlocked the kitchen door and both used their hands to guide them along the wall and up into his bedroom. The curtains overlooking the balcony were drawn. Kuan Hee peeked through a slit at the edge of the curtains. Street lamps illuminated the lane in front of the house. There wasn't a soul out there. No cars too. *They can't be watching my house twenty-four seven*, he thought. *Maybe they installed a camera outside.* He surveyed the lamp posts and the street sign. *Nothing*, he told himself.

"Are we sleeping here or in the cellar?"

The light from the street lamps helped illuminate the part of the bedroom next to the curtains.

"We can't use the air-conditioning."

"I know. So here or down in the cellar?"

"We'll go down when the situation get bad."

"OK. I'll jump in first."

"Kuan Hee."

"Yes?"

"When are we having children?"

"You don't make sense, you know. My parents are in trouble and we are hiding here. Is that all you can think about?"

"Aw, don't be mean. I was merely asking—for fun."

"It's not my idea of fun."

"Kuan Hee."

"What?"

"I don't want children."

"You just said you wanted children and now you are saying the opposite—make up your mind, please."

"When did I say I want children?"

"Just now—a minute ago."

"No *lah*. I was only wondering whether we will have children. It doesn't mean I want children."

"OIC. You mean we aren't going to have children?"

"I want to wait. I have seen these girls in my block. They are slim and pretty. But after they get married and have children—their bellies swell. Can't wear body-hugging jeans any more. And the cellulite on the back of their hips—eek!" There was no response from Kuan Hee.

She elbowed him. "Kuan Hee."

"Mmm."

"Weren't you listening?"

"I—I was. But, I was also thinking about my parents."

"Things will turn out well."

"Hope so."

Lina flashed him a cheeky look. Her eyes told it all. She wanted—.

"It's warm inside. Come right in."

"You are heavy."

"I'm not. You're bony, that's why. Can't even take my weight. Fancy a little thing on top of you—and you go complaining."

"I'm only afraid—it will break."

"So strong, how to break. See?"

"Aw. Don't grab so hard, can or not."

"Serve you right. If you don't know what to say—shut

up."

"Sorry, dear."

"Don't grip my breasts so hard, lah."

"Like that can?"

"Kiss me. Kiss me."

"Your hair's all over my face. Very ticklish. Need to breathe; don't press my lips so hard. My ears—don't use too much force."

"Kuan Hee, I love you."

"I know."

"Say you love me."

"I love you."

"Again."

"I love you. It's coming out. Quick. Get off—I need to pull it ou—"

"It's all over your body and my thighs."

"Too late—couldn't stop it."

"Kuan Hee, I want you to sleep naked tonight."

"Mmm."

CHAPTER 15

A popular saying goes like this:

After the rain comes sunshine.

It had been raining cats and dogs for the past two days. *When will sunshine come back into my life?* wondered Kuan Hee. He didn't say it aloud, for he was afraid Lina would misunderstand him. Of course, Lina was his sunshine; so were his parents. He wasn't thinking about her; he was thinking about his parents. *What if they use torture? Can my parents survive the ordeal?* he wondered.

His father once told him that worms came to the surface during heavy rain. He had explained that the water made the worms moist so they could easily move to a new location to escape predators. *Can we...will we get a chance to escape to a new place...a new life?* he wondered. Then he remembered Lina. *With Lina, of course, all four of them,* he thought.

Were his thoughts sending out cryptic messages to him? He could not decide. A voice in his head was speaking to him now. It interrupted his train of thought. It was his father. He wanted Kuan Hee to meet him somewhere—now. There was great urgency in his voice. His father had terse instructions for him; he told Kuan Hee to shut up and listen when Kuan Hee kept asking questions.

Kuan Hee grabbed his Crumpler bag. "We need to move now. Grab your backpack."

"Where to?"

He reached for Lina's hand. "Just follow me." They descended the stairs and made for the front gate.

"That's the front gate."

"Never mind. No time to use the back. Hurry."

Reluctantly, Lina tagged along. On Upper Serangoon Road, Kuan Hee hailed a taxi and they got in.

"Bukit Timah Plaza," he said to the taxi driver.

Upon arrival, Kuan Hee asked the driver to let them alight along Jalan Anak Bukit. Then he paid the driver and they got off. He waited a few minutes, till the taxi had disappeared from view. Then he grabbed Lina's hand and ran across the road with her. He was careful to avoid the road junction—there were cameras overhead. All this while he did not say a single word. When Lina protested, he merely put flicked a finger onto his mouth. She understood immediately.

The pair walked down Dunearn Road and turned into Rifle Range Road. They moved along the perimeter of a firing range. After a fifteen-minute walk, they found themselves near a building. A sign read:

Temasek Officers' Mess

The place was deserted. The building was dilapidated. It seemed nobody had taken care of the premises for some time. Grass was creeping onto the front porch. It had populated every nook and crevice in the area. The windows were nailed shut with timber planks. The paintwork was peeling off from the walls; there were pockets of air bubbles in it. Whatever grandeur the building might have had in the past, it showed no trace of it now.

Kuan Hee led the way along the edge of the building. Soon they came to a narrow passageway—it separated the main building from the narrow one behind. He opened a door at the far end of the narrow building—it creaked as it swung open. They stepped into a narrow corridor and came to an enfilade of rooms.

"Dad. Mum."

"Uncle. Auntie."

There was a noise in one room. Then the elder Wang appeared in its doorway. He waved them into the room. There they were—his father and mother—standing in front of him. He hugged them one by one. They hugged him. Then they hugged each other. Lina was in tears. The moment was too much for her.

"Come sit down and talk," said his father. He motioned for the pair to sit on a pile of wooden pallets. His parents sat on wooden crates. Their buttocks pressed on the rough grainy surface of the makeshift chairs.

"Kuan Hee, listen carefully," said his father. "We need to get out of the island as quickly as we can."

"How did you guys escape?" said Kuan Hee.

"It's a long story. In a nutshell, we scooted off when the people guarding us were distracted," said his father.

"Yes, it was like a miracle," said his mother. "Almost a miracle."

"How did you get out of the building?"

"Well, it wasn't the same building that they put us in at first," said his father. "I had complained that I did not have my tools and instruments. They relented and moved us to my workplace."

"Yes, it was easy for your father there," said his mother.

"Yes. I know the place like the back of my hand. I have access to all parts of the complex," said his father.

"How did you get here?" asked Kuan Hee.

"Let your father speak his piece," said his mother.

"We came in a taxi. As a young man, I used to frequent this place. In this room, I spent many hours reading my research notes and chatting with friends," said his father. "That's why I came here. I am relaxed here. I feel at home here. I think better here." His father paused to collect his thoughts.

"I have contacted a good friend. He's willing to help," said his father. "He has arranged for a boat near Coney Island tonight. It will take us to Pasir Gudam in Johor Bahru."

His father paused again. Then he continued. "I have spoken to the Americans. They are happy to have me working for them. We will take a taxi from Pasir Gudam to Kuala Lumpur. Airport. From there, we will board a USAF plane which will take us to Geraldton in Western Australia. That's where the American spy base is located."

"Dad, why can't we simply go into the American Embassy? Like in the movies," said Kuan Hee.

"They may take us down before we even step foot in the embassy," said his father. "There are G men stationed outside the embassy twenty-four seven. I can't take the risk—not with your mother around."

"Can you trust this friend of yours?" asked his mother.

"We have been friends since schooldays. He's my schoolmate at Victoria School."

"But Dad, people have been telling on one another, ever since the regime took power," said Kuan Hee.

"I have no choice," said his father. "It's a risk we have to take. Anyway, it's set. We need to get ready for the journey."

"Lina, you can't come with us," said Kuan Hee

"Yes, Lina, Kuan Hee is right," said his mother. "We can't take you along."

"I understand, Auntie," said Lina. She was also sure her mother would never let her leave Singapore with Kuan Hee.

Lina was glad they had had their little tryst two days ago. She didn't know when they could be together again. Australia was nine hours of plane ride away. She would miss Kuan Hee dearly. The pair retreated to a corner in the room and cuddled each other. Who knew when they could feel each other's warm embrace again? They were resigned to their fate.

CHAPTER 16

The moon looked big and round tonight. It was smiling down at the four dark figures treading along sparsely illuminated Rifle Range Road towards Dunearn Road. Was it telling them everything would go as smoothly as its surface? Kuan Hee, his parents, and Lina were busy thinking about what lay ahead for them the next few weeks—and months too. They did not have the time to take in the view.

A taxi took them to Edgefield Plains in Punggol. They alighted on the side of the road, careful not to be in view of the cameras in the HDB blocks. Then they walked along Punggol Nature Walk towards the west entrance of Coney Island. The promenade was deserted; occasionally, two or three joggers would pass them. They could see the entire south side of Coney Island from where they were. There was a police post at the head of the Nature Walk, a ten-minute walk away. They had to keep away from the post.

Soon they came to a sheltered rest-stop. It was where they would meet the boat. There was no sign of it in the distance. Above them, the moon seemed to be watching them; it was illuminating their surroundings. It was quiet out here.

The chugging of an engine punctured the silence. First, faint sounds, then loud droning sounds. Then it appeared in the distance. The boat slowed as power to its engine was cut off. It drifted close to the edge of the promenade and a man in it jumped onshore. Using a rope, he pulled it against the embankment, then beckoned the passengers to board. The elder Wang boarded the boat first, then he helped his wife into the boat. It was Kuan Hee's turn. He was heavy-hearted; Lina was emotional. She was on the verge of crying. But she held back the tears. She wanted to look strong in front of Kuan Hee today.

"Kuan Hee, Say your goodbyes; the boat is leaving," said his father.

"I'll miss you, bye," said Kuan Hee.

"Don't forget me. Don't ever forget me," said Lina.

The boat's engine roared into life and the boat moved away from the embankment. The Wang family waved at Lina. She waved back.

Suddenly, a voice boomed over a loudspeaker.

"Stop! Stop! Coastguard," said the voice.

A patrol boat came into view. There were soldiers—not policemen—in it. They looked menacing.

"Kuan Hee, quick, jump into the water," said his father.

"No Dad, no. I can't leave you and Mum," said Kuan Hee.

"Jump now, or it will be too late," screamed his father. It was the first time his father was screaming at him. His father had to be real mad this time.

"But—" It was too late for words; his father had pushed Kuan Hee overboard.

"Swim. Swim quickly," said his father.

"Kuan Hee, take care of yourself," said his mother.

Recovering from the initial shock, Kuan Hee swam towards the shore—to where Lina was standing. He wanted to stop and take a look at his parents, but he couldn't. The patrol boat was faster than his little body. He could fall into their hands. And his parents would be sorely disappointed with him. He fought back the tears in the water and swam with all his might.

On the embankment, Lina helped Kuan Hee up. They took a long look at the silhouette of the two boats. It was to have been a happy day for the Wang family. *How did it end up this way?* Kuan Hee wondered. Lina pulled him away from the shore. It was dangerous for them to remain in the area. The G men could come for him any moment.

CHAPTER 17

Kuan Hee was now determined. He had to find out where the G men had taken his parents. He had to get them out. The person who had knowledge of their whereabouts was Colonel Tee. The place to get information from him was Belmont Road.

Kuan Hee and Lina sat on the grassy verge on the side of the road. They had come prepared with folding stools this time. It was a brooding Kuan Hee who stabbed at the drawing block with his pencil. His parents' capture by the G men was still fresh in his mind.

Lina touched his wrist. And his thoughts returned to the present. He released Busy the housefly into the air and flipped open a remote-control card.

The titanium housefly flitted over the plainclothes in the garden, into the living room. They were in luck— Colonel Tee was seated in a big armchair next to the coffee table. Mrs Tee was walking into the room. She was carrying a tray of pastries and coffee or tea.

Busy the housefly landed on a picture frame next to the verandah doorway.

There was nothing interesting—they were having small talk. The minutes wore on. Evidently, Colonel Tee did not discuss work with his wife. Inside the house, the Tee couple were having coffee. On the roadside, Kuan Hee and Lina were watching for mosquitoes. The pests had taken some bites out of the pair.

It is another fruitless day, the pair thought. Lina suggested they fly little Busy up into the bedrooms to see if Jordan was in. Busy the housefly was flitting through the living room when the pair saw Colonel Tee rising from his seat. Mrs Tee passed him an attaché case and he left the house. Kuan Hee had a change of mind. He commanded little Busy to fly after him. Colonel Tee got into a Mercedes and the car moved down the driveway. Little Busy had perched itself on an antenna at the back of the car. The car was now moving out of Belmont Road.

"It's going out of range, Kuan Hee."

Kuan Hee pointed at the sky. "No, it won't—see? Satellite. That's what the fly relies on. It'll never go out of range. That's what Dad says."

It was a short journey. The Mercedes cruised down Holland Road with bodyguards in two Volvos—one behind and one in front, moving under the flyover to the lower part of the thoroughfare. The convoy continued down the road and turned into—Gleneagles Hospital! Colonel Tee wasn't going to work.

Is he visiting someone, Jordan, perhaps? wondered the pair.

Colonel Tee and his bodyguards entered a suite on the third level. There were more plainclothes waiting for them there.

In an office, stood three men in clinical white.

"They must be doctors," Kuan Hee.

Colonel Tee wore a grave look. He listened intently as the doctors, one by one, delivered their prognosis.

Who are they talking about? Is it Jordan? the pair wondered.

The doctors told Colonel Tee his prospects of recovering from advanced leukemia was poor. He learnt he had at most six months to live.

It is not Jordan, after all, but the dictator himself, the pair thought.

After the doctors had sworn to keep the prognosis a secret, Colonel Tee and his minders left with Busy the housefly hovering above them.

The convoy moved on the opposite side of Holland Road and turned left into Minden Road and then Sherwood Road. The passengers disembarked at the front of a large building. A large sign read:

Prime Minister's Office

But, the PMO was at the back of the Istana. *Has it moved here?* wondered the pair. *When?*

A small sign on a pillar of the building read:

Tanglin Complex

The Tanglin Complex had housed the Ministry of Defence back in the 1970s and 1980s. It was now supposed to be the address of the Ministry of Foreign Affairs. Kuan Hee and Lina sat bewildered. They were oblivious to the lady walking her three dogs on the other side of the road. The dogs' barking woke them from their thoughts. They had to get out of the place, for the barks were drawing the attention of men in the garden above them. The pair ran towards the main road, with hands clutching drawing boards and pencils.

Tanglin Complex was within walking distance. The pair had been sitting on the grass for ages and it was good exercise for them to walk to the building. Also, boarding a bus might mean they would be monitored by cameras on the bus.

As they made their way down the lower part of Holland Road, they kept their eyes on the small remote-control screen. In their haste to get out of Cornwall Gardens, they had no time to monitor Colonel Tee.

Apparently, Colonel Tee was in a bad mood today. In

his office, he kept reprimanding his subordinates. His minders were careful to keep some distance between him and them.

By this time, Kuan Hee and Lina had reached the beginning of Minden Road. There were sentries at a guard post thirty metres ahead of them. A metal barrier gate floated a metre above the tarmac. Tanglin Complex was visible from the main road. It was sitting on top of the slope.

The pair decided to take up position on the roadside. They reprised their routine, pretending to draw Tanglin Complex.

Busy the housefly was atop an air-conditioning unit in Colonel Tee's office. The room was longish, spanning the entire width of the building. Colonel Tee sat hunched behind a huge wooden desk, against a window with its curtains drawn. He was alone. The room was dim, with only the light from a table lamp on the table to illuminate it. But, it was bright daylight outside.

It was apparent Colonel Tee did not like bright places. The door opened and a female soldier walked in. She held it open and some men came in. There was a disheveled man between two burly plain clothes.

"It—it's Father," Kuan Hee.

The pair glued their eyes to the screen. They had stopped pretending to draw.

"Professor Wang, what is your answer?" said Colonel Tee.

The voice came crisp and clear through the small speakers of the remote.

"I refuse to do your bidding," said Kuan Hee's father. "You can't force me to do things against my will. This is a democracy."

"Professor Wang. This is indeed a democracy. It's my kind of democracy—my kind of rule," said Colonel Tee. "Don't you want your wife to go free?"

"You are worse than an animal," said Kuan Hee's

father. "You're a beast."

"Call me what you want. Any names also can," said Colonel Tee. "I don't care—as long as you agree."

Just what does he want Dad to agree to? wondered Kuan Hee.

"Soon your family will be complete," said Colonel Tee. "I have men looking for your son—Kuan Hee. Is that his name?"

"Don't you dare lay your filthy hands on my son," said Kuan Hee's father. "Don't you dare."

"You care about your son, right?" said Colonel Tee. "I have a son, too." He paused.

"I'll give you another day to think over," said Colonel Tee. "Just one more day—but, don't test my patience."

He flicked a finger and his men removed Kuan Hee's father from his room.

"You are a beast! You don't give a damn about your son," screamed Kuan Hee's father.

"Dad, Dad," said Kuan Hee.

But his father could not hear him. Colonel Tee couldn't hear him either. Lina leaned her head against Huan Hee's shoulder. Then he remembered where he was—on the roadside.

Kuan Hee's eyes were red. He was tearful. The moment had been heartrending. He could see his father on the screen, but he was helpless to him. Lina consoled him.

"Things will get better, don't worry." Then she stiffened. "Quick. Follow your father."

Kuan Hee dispatched Busy the housefly after the men. They were nowhere to be seen. Alas! He had been distracted. He blamed himself. Little Busy flitted through the corridors of the building and then out into the compound.

They couldn't have disappeared so quickly, Kuan Hee thought. *I had taken my eyes off them for only a few seconds.*

Then the pair saw his father and his guards. They had come out of a doorway at the far end. They bundled him into a minibus. Kuan Hee sent Busy the housefly after them. The metallic housefly attached itself to the top of the minibus as it was moving out of the compound.

"Are we going to follow them?"

"No need. Little Busy has got GPS capability."

Today, the pair had learnt some new things. Chief was that his father was alright. He appeared unharmed. Next was that Colonel Tee was dying soon—in a matter of months.

His dictatorship is to be short-lived, they thought. *Soon, Singapore will be free again.*

The pair still did not know what Colonel Tee wanted Kuan Hee's father to do for him. And they were soon going to find out where the G men were holding his parents.

"Let's pack up."

"Aren't we going to find out more?"

"No need. He can't run away. We know he's here. We can always come back."

"Where are we going?"

"To find my parents, but first, let's quench our thirst."

CHAPTER 18

The red dot was flashing on the remote-control screen. But, it was no longer moving. Busy the housefly had arrived at the place where the G men had taken Kuan Hee's father.

The map showed Maju Camp next to the red dot. It was situated on a grassy patch of land just behind Ngee Ann Polytechnic in Clementi.

Kuan Hee and Lina were enjoying a cold drink at nearby Tanglin Mall. They had spent hours in the sun today. They ordered some food to go.

"It's quite near Temasek Officers' Mess. About eight hundred metres away. I need to go there right away."

"I know. I want to tag along."

A taxi took the pair to Maju Drive. They alighted about fifty metres from the camp and trudged up the road, at times peering into the camp through the perimeter fencing. Cables running along the middle of the fence told Kuan Hee the fence was electrified. Ahead, the perimeter fencing parted at a road opening which was guarded by armed soldiers—not a single fresh face, all regulars. A metal barrier gate cordoned off the road, which led to two large single-storey buildings standing parallel to each other about a hundred metres away.

The flashing dot on the screen showed little Busy was between the two buildings. The buildings were longish with casement windows and a sloping tiled roof. The bottom quarter of the walls consisted of red bricks. The upper portion was whitewashed. Cameras were mounted on the corners of the building. No doors were seen on the side facing the road. Soon it would be nightfall and cold air would envelop the surrounding area. The pair had not come prepared for an overnight stay.

"Can you get little Busy to give us a view of the surroundings?"

"Let me get to the live screen."

"Doesn't little Busy run out of juice? It's been ages since we activated it."

"It's got tiny solar panels wrapped over its body."

"You mean—so many? Tinier than tiny little Busy?"

"Yes. That's what Dad said."

"Where is little Busy now?"

"It's still on the minibus. Shall we get it to start work?"

Little Busy flitted into life. It flew along the open space between the two identical buildings. There were four sets of double-louvered doors along each building. The doors sat between casement windows. Two armed soldiers—regulars—stood guard at the doorway in the middle of the first building.

Could Dad be in the first building? wondered Kuan Hee.

Kuan Hee piloted little Busy through the louvres into the building. There were men in white lab coats shuffling along the corridor. On one side of the corridor were doors.

Which one should I try first? wondered Kuan Hee.

Little Busy turned right and flitted to the farthest door. There was no opening either under the door or above it. It went from door to door—there were no openings anywhere.

How is little Busy going to look into the rooms? wondered

Kuan Hee.

"Look, someone is coming out of a room."

"I'll get little Busy to follow him."

Little Busy flitted into a room with a man in white lab coat. It seemed to be a laboratory of some kind. There were cupboards lining the walls and sophisticated equipment on a large counter top in the centre of the room. Two men were at work in the room. One was peering through a microscope.

"Negative here. We'll have to wait till someone enters or leaves."

It was a good hour's wait. It was cold out in the open, and the pair were famished. They chomped on the Big Macs they had bought at Tanglin Mall.

"Are we really going to barge into the place to rescue your parents?"

"If they are in there, of course, I am."

"But, we—we are alone. We don't have support. We are unarmed."

"Don't forget these two—he opened his backpack and AleXander's heads popped out."

Lina looked amused. She still didn't believe these two toy robots could be that lethal.

"Look! The door is opening."

Little Busy flitted through the door into the corridor. Two armed soldiers were making their rounds. They did not enter any of the rooms.

Then a soldier came in from the front door. He was carrying some food boxes. Little Busy flew above him as he made a turn and knocked a door. The door opened and both went in. The room was about the size of a four-roomed HDB flat. There were at least a dozen servers in cabinets along the walls. There were computer monitors on a big table on the left and in the middle sat a circular glass enclosure—something like the capsule lift in Wisma Atria, only bigger. An armchair was in the capsule. Overhead was what looked like an oversized coat hanger on a metal stand. It had thick cables fanning out of it, and dangling in the air.

There was no sign of Kuan Hee's father or mother. Only a lone soldier who was now chatting with his comrade. He took a food box to what seemed to be a pantry while the other sat at the table eating his dinner. Then he returned to join the soldier. Both were now partaking of their food.

"Kuan Hee, get little Busy to go into the side room. There's someone in there. The soldier came out without the food box."

Little Busy's wings flapped busily as it flew into the pantry. It wasn't a pantry—it was a small office. There it hovered over the cabinet and—someone in a chair.

"It's Dad."

"Go nearer. Go nearer."

The elder Wang looked sullen. He was unshaved and his eyes had dark circles under them. He was slouched over an office chair. His arms were on the armrests—but they were not restrained. The food box lay unopened on a desk next to him.

Little Busy swooped down to his ears.

Kuan Hee spoke into the microphone on the remote. "Dad, Dad."

His father roused. He looked dazed. Then he saw little Busy. "Son."

"Dad, are you alright?"

"Yes son. How did you know I'm here?"

"We followed you from Colonel Tee's office."

"You did? Where are you now?"

"Outside—down the road. Where's Mum."

"I don't know—she's not with me, son. I don't know where they have taken her."

There was an awkward silence, for they had heard the shuffling of feet. A soldier appeared at the doorway. He had thought he heard something. *Must be talking to himself,* the soldier thought. Seeing nothing was amiss, he returned to his partner.

"Dad, I'm going to get you out."

"How? You are alone and these are professionals—rangers, not NSmen."

"I've brought AleXander with me."

"No, wait, son. You can't—not now. If they find me gone, there's no telling what they will do to your mum. You can't."

There was silence on Kuan Hee's side. He was stupefied—he did not know what to say to his father.

"Son, I want you to do something for me."

"Yes, Dad."

"Listen carefully, go to the American Embassy—don't visit them. Don't call them. Don't e-mail them. Use the chat on their Website. It's encrypted and safe. Ask for Brigadier Walmsley of Special Forces, Department of Defence. His name is James Walmsley. J-a-m-e-s. W-a-l-m-s-l-e-y. You got that?"

"Lina has scribbled down the name."

"She's with you?"

"Yes."

"Good. When he contacts you, tell him what has happened to me. Tell him everything. Ask him to get your mum and me out."

"Do they know where Mum is?"

"They have the means. They are Delta Force."

"Tell him—Colonel Tee is dying. He won't live past this year. Tel—"

"I know that news, Dad."

"You do? How—never mind. Listen, don't interrupt. Tell him Colonel Tee wants me to let him live in another person's body. Tell him he wants me to do it these few days. Tell him to act fast. You got all that down, son?"

"Lina, all jotted down?"

"Yes."

"Yes, Dad."

"Good. Now get out of here. You can't do anything for

me here. Go find Brigadier Walmsley. Go find your mother."

"Yes, Dad—take care of yourself, Dad."

"Uncle, please eat something. You need to be strong."

"I will. I will. Now go. Kuan Hee, leave the housefly with me. Go to the remote's main menu. Set it to 'Others', then 'Voice Command'."

"All done, Dad."

CHAPTER 19

In Hougang Bus Interchange, Kuan Hee and Lina loitered, keeping an eye out for a bearded old Caucasian wearing a hunting hat. That was how Brigadier Walmsley had described himself.

There he was, standing next to the Buzz Convenient Store. He was much taller than Kuan Hee. They greeted each other and strolled across the road towards Hougang Mall. Along the way, the Brigadier fanned himself with his hat, complaining about the hot weather in Singapore.

At ToastBox in basement one, Kuan Hee and Lina sat next to each other, with the Brigadier facing Kuan Hee.

The Brigadier had both arms on the table. He asked for *kopi oh kosong*. He seemed to know some *Singlish*.

"I am curious—why did you guys move out of Sembawang?"

"Your previous government didn't want to anger the Chinese," said Brigadier Walmsley. "It wanted to show to the world it was neutral. So—we had to get out—move to Australia."

As the Brigadier sat twiddling his thumbs, he recounted the times he had spent in Singapore—in his youth mostly. He had also worked at the American airbase in

Sembawang.

Kuan Hee felt the Brigadier was just making small talk; he was actually sizing up the surroundings—to see if there were spies in their midst. He was ever so careful in his casual ways.

"I'm sorry to hear about your Dad."

"Thank you, Mr Walmsley, for your concern."

"Call me James. Everyone calls me that."

"Yes, Mr Walmsley."

"Your father is a rare breed. Talented—immensely talented."

Kuan Hee blushed. It was the first time he had heard someone heaping praises upon his father.

"Here, come closer." He hunched over the table and Kuan Hee did the same. Then Kuan Hee felt something touch his knee.

"Take this." The Brigadier passed something to Kuan Hee under the table. It felt like paper—folded paper and a candy-bar shaped thing, with a protruding rod, probably metal—it was cold to the touch. Kuan Hee quickly pocketed them.

"This is how we get in touch from now on."

Kuan Hee nodded, though he didn't quite understand how they would get in touch. He inferred it had something to do with the things in his pocket. *Perhaps, the Brigadier doesn't want others to hear, just in case someone is eavesdropping,* Kuan Hee thought.

Near Hougang MRT Station, the pair bade farewell to the Brigadier. He had come in a taxi, but wanted to take a ride back to the embassy on the MRT.

"Don't worry, your father will be OK. And your Mum too."

"Thank you, Mr Walmsley."

In his bedroom, Kuan Hee emptied his pocket. The candle-bar thing was a walkie-talkie. It was slightly bigger than the palm of his hands. The other thing was a folded note. He opened the paper. The typed text read:

> **This walkie-talkie has a range of one hundred kilometres. It works anywhere in Singapore. Use it to talk to me. It is linked to a satellite. Everything is encrypted. Set to Channel three. Keep it safe.**

"The Brigadier didn't say much."

"He's being careful. He's an old hand at such things. But he said enough."

"What's next, Kuan Hee?"

"Get something to eat. Come. Let's go down to the kitchen."

The pair clambered down the dark stairs. Having had plenty of practice the past weeks, they were sure-footed— they could almost move around the dark house blind-folded. It was plain Maggie mee for the pair again, for they had run out of eggs.

"Little Busy is no longer with us. Poor big Tizzy is going to be lonely."

"Yeah. I guess so. But Dad needs little Busy more than we need it."

"Are we going to find your mother?"

"Why do you ask?"

"The Brigadier said he would help us, didn't he?"

"Isn't it better if both sides try?"

"How are we going to find your mother?"

"Guess it is by spying on Colonel Tee again."

"Are we going to Tanglin Complex again?"

"Looks like it."

CHAPTER 20

A famous saying goes:

All men think all men mortal, but themselves.

Colonel Tee believed in power—seizing it and holding on to it by force. He knew man was mortal, but he had forgotten he was mortal too. Perhaps, he thought he could live forever, but through human existence on earth, what man had succeeded in cheating death? History held numerous examples. Emperor Shih Huang Ti sought the elixir of immortality, but failed to escape death. Colonel Tee, likewise, wanted a long life to enjoy the power he had amassed. Alas, he had forgotten the adage:

What man proposes, God disposes.

Colonel Tee was dying. To remain powerful, he had to live. Was there such a Holy Grail? If there were, then Kuan Hee's father held the key to it. Colonel Tee knew Professor Wang was the one man who could let him carry on living—albeit in another person's body. He was willing to pay any price to satisfy his ego. He would even sacrifice his own son.

Professor Wang had been ordered to carry out an operation to transfer Colonel Tee's memories to another person's brain. Colonel Tee's son, Jordan made a good specimen. Colonel Tee would live in his son's body. It was akin to the Hermit Crab which salvages an empty snail shell to use as its home.

Jordan is my own flesh and blood, so power would still lie in the Tee family, Colonel Tee had reasoned to himself. *My son and I would become one soon.*

Colonel Tee had grand plans for the professor to execute for him. Moving forward, Colonel Tee wanted Professor Wang to speed up his nanotechnology research on reproductive cloning of human beings. Though it was ten to twenty years before this would become feasible, he was sure Professor Wang could do it in double time. That was why Professor Wang was so important to Colonel Tee.

The Tee Dynasty should not end with me and my son, Colonel Tee thought. *It should go on perpetually.*

Professor Wang was a brilliant scientist. *He could replicate my son's body and my memories repeatedly,* Colonel Tee thought. *This way, we would live forever, and hold power indefinitely—Father and son.*

Colonel Tee had forgotten Professor Wang was a mortal. Professor Wang would certainly not be by his side for eternity.

"He hasn't bated an eyelid in ages. Is he dead?"

"I think he's in deep thought."

"Why are things going so slowly today?"

"Don't be impatient."

Kuan Hee and Lina had stationed themselves at the road junction where a lane of traffic filtered into Holland Road. This time they took on the role of survey staff. They sat on the grass clicking on counters as the cars moved past them.

"Kuan Hee, the sky is getting dark. It's going to rain

soon."

"Shush."

Colonel Tee had stirred in his armchair. Someone had entered his room. He was waiting for Colonel Tee to wake.

"Sir, Sir," said the man in a low tone. Tizzy the dragonfly flitted over the man. In the dim light, Kuan Hee could make out the emblems on his epaulettes. One crest. He was a major.

"Sir," said the major. The volume was louder now.

"Whaaat?" The Colonel had wakened.

"Sir, it is ready."

"Oh. So he's finally agreed, hasn't he."

"Yes, sir."

"Thursday then."

"This Thursday, sir?"

"Yes. Let's do it first thing in the morning. 8:00 a.m."

"Yes, sir."

"What's that thing?"

"What, sir?"

"On the wall behind you."

"I—I think it's a dragonfly, sir."

"Drat. These pesky insects. Ask my secretary to get someone to get rid of it."

"Yes, sir."

Before the major could speak to the colonel's secretary, little Dragonfly had scooted out of the room. It was now flying back to the pair.

"I told you, big Tizzy is too big for a spy job."

"Never mind. Let's close shop for today."

With big Tizzy safely in their hands, the pair walked towards Tanglin Mall.

"I think he is talking about my father."

"I think so too."

"So—the operation will take place in three days' time. I've got to tell the Brigadier."

"What if we are wrong?"

"It's got to be it. We can't be wrong."

The pair were now in an open space outside Tanglin Mall. Bringing out the walkie-talkie, Kuan Hee pressed the push-to-talk button.

"Calling Mr Walmsley. Calling Mr Walmsley. Over."

"Yes, Kuan Hee. This is James. Over."

"Mr Walmsley. Colonel Tee's operation will take place on Thursday at 8:00 a.m. Over."

"How did you know, Kuan Hee? Over."

"I overheard him telling a major. Over."

"I see. You were with the colonel? Over."

"No, Mr Walmsley. But Tizzy was in the room with him. Over."

"Tizzy? Over."

"Yes. Mr Walmsley. Tizzy the dragonfly—I mean the titanium dragonfly my father invented. Eh. Over."

"Yes. I see what you mean. Tizzy is a drone robot. Over."

"Yes, Mr Walmsley. Using a remote-control device, I can see and hear what it sees and hears. Over."

"So Colonel Tee said Thursday 8:00 a.m. Is that it? Over."

"Yes, that's correct. Mr Walmsley. Over."

"OK. I got it. Thanks very much, Kuan Hee. I appreciate it. I will get things going. Not to worry. By the way, we've found your mother. Over."

"Really? That's great. How's my mum? Over."

"My guys say she is well. Not harmed. Over."

"Thank you very much. Mr Walmsley. Over."

"We'll take her to safety soon, Kuan Hee. Over."

"Thank you, Mr Walmsley. Over."

"That's it then, Kuan Hee. Bye for now. Over."

Such a polite young man, thought the Brigadier as he put away the walkie-talkie. *Takes after his father.*

"Bye bye, Mr Walmsley. Over."

"It's good news, Kuan Hee."

"Yes, it is." Kuan Hee was beaming. "It's been a long time coming. I've been waiting too long for this moment."

CHAPTER 21

It was late evening. The air over Maju Camp was cold and a blustery wind was sweeping the open field where Kuan Hee and Lina sat huddled. They had come because Kuan Hee wanted to tell his father the good news about his mother. He could have used the embedded device in his arm, but he also wanted to take a look at his father—to see if he was doing fine. Maju Camp was the place to be.

The pair had come prepared to spend the night there. *We and your father are near each other tonight—that's what's important,* Lina thought as she leaned against Kuan Hee.

Kuan Hee had awakened little Busy. It wriggled out of the elder Wang's pocket and darted into the air. His father was taking a nap in the room. His eyes were shut, and he didn't stir when little Busy was buzzing in his pocket.

"Let's not wake your father. Let him sleep."

"Yes. He hasn't had a good rest for some time. Dad seldom sleeps like this. He must be dead tired."

"Look around the room, Kuan Hee."

Little Busy flew out into the main room and took in the view of the surroundings. The same two guards were sitting at the table, playing a card game. Their rifles were resting on the wall next to them. The room was crowded with equipment now. There were two motorized gurneys at one of the walls.

"Looks like they are getting the place ready for some big thing. Probably going to hold the operation here."

"You mean the one on Colonel Tee—tomorrow morning?"

"Yes. If the Brigadier's men do not take action by tonight, then Colonel Tee will live in a new body—Jordan's."

"It's so quiet here. I doubt anything will happen tonight."

"Commandoes like to do their thing just before dawn—when people are bound to be asleep or falling asleep."

"How do you know?"

"The movies, my dear. The movies."

Suddenly, the sky above them roared. A large dark object was hovering over the building.

"It looks like an Apache!"

"Quick. Let's take a closer look."

Some dark figures were rappelling down ropes dangling from the attack helicopter. There were only a handful of them—eight, perhaps. No. There were six. As they descended, they fired their sub-machine guns from their hips. Some soldiers on the ground were firing back. The firefight was deafening in the silence of the night. Soldiers were shouting and the sound of running boots was heard. An armored personnel carrier roared into life in the distance. A soldier atop the carrier fired at the intruders.

Within the room, the elder Wang had awakened. His minders were ushering him out into the corridor, rifles slung. Little Busy flitted after them. There were soldiers running in the corridor. Many were holding their rifles in their hands. Someone was shouting orders. As the soldiers ran out into the compound, some were gunned down by the intruders. Others retreated behind the door. In the corridor, above the soldiers, an intruder fired into the soldiers, knocking them down with precision. This commando took two shots at the soldiers with the elder Wang. They fell to the ground; they didn't even have time to unsling their rifles. They were not rangers after all—just plain clumsy regulars.

The remaining soldiers in the corridor fell one after another as other commandoes entered the building. Two commandoes grabbed the elder Wang and they scurried out of the building. Another two were in the compound watching the area. Two were engaged in a firefight with the armored personnel carrier. It was commandoes against armor. The rumbling of a heavy vehicle could be heard from behind the armored personnel carrier. A Leopard tank was lumbering towards the commandoes. There were a score of soldiers at its side. They fanned out across the two buildings.

The whole area was noisy and chaotic. The Apache was now hovering almost a metre above ground some thirty metres away in the open field.

The two commandoes and the elder Wang ran into the field, with another two close behind, covering their back. The last two commandoes lobbed some grenades at the armored personnel carrier and the tank. They too ran in the direction of the Apache.

It was almost like in the movies. Except this was for real. The cranking of the tank's cannon could be heard. Then a loud boom echoed through the air. The tank was firing at the Apache. It was like a sitting duck!

By now the armored personnel carrier had rolled into the open field. Its machine gun fired furiously at the commandoes. A commando dropped onto the ground. Another grabbed him and together they hobbled towards the Apache. The elder Wang was hit. So was the commando next to him. Two commandoes helped them into the Apache. The last two commandoes to board stood on a metal bar outside the helicopter which fanned the ground as it rose into the air.

Now the Apache was ready to take on the armored personnel carrier. It shot a rocket at the carrier, disabling it. The soldier atop the carrier was nowhere to be seen. Plumes of smoke were billowing from the top of the carrier.

The tank appeared at the side of the carrier. It cranked its cannon skywards taking aim at the Apache. But the Apache was now in its element. It promptly dispatched two anti-tank missiles at the tank, sending it up in balls of flames and plumes of smoke. It shot another two rockets at the first building, opening big gaping holes in its side. Apparently, it was targeting the laboratory where the elder Wang had been held.

All the while little Busy was perched on a louvred door, taking in the happenings and sending them to Kuan Hee and Lina.

"Dad's injured. Dad's injured."

Lina was wailing. "What shall we do? What shall we do?"

Kuan Hee wiped off his tears with a hand. He was emotional. He had to breathe hard and deeply. He had to calm down and collect his rampant thoughts.

Turning to Lina, he clutched her arm.

"We've got to get out of here. It will be crawling with soldiers soon."

"What?" Lina had yet to compose herself. She looked bewildered.

"Busy—got to get Busy back." He tapped furiously on the remote.

Then they ran into the darkness, with the buildings, the tank and the armored personnel carrier burning behind them.

CHAPTER 22

The walkie-talkie crackled into life. The Brigadier was calling Kuan Hee. Kuan Hee and Lina were now in the dimly lit open space outside Bukit Timah Plaza. The flyover towered overhead. They had run all the way from Maju Camp and were now taking a breather. They thought they were safe here.

"Kuan Hee, your father's safely with us. Over."

"Mr Walmsley. Is he badly injured? Over."

"How did you know? I was about to tell you. Over."

"I was there—in the field, watching the whole thing unfold. Over."

"I see. Your father is being fetched to a hospital on board our ship. I am told he was shot in the chest. But, not to worry, it's not near the heart. Over."

"Is he conscious? Can he talk? Does he respond? Over."

"He is unconscious now. But don't worry. We have the best medical equipment on board. He'll be fine. Over."

"Thank you very much, Mr Walmsley. Over."

"Another thing—your mum is also safe in our hands. Over."

"Is she? That's good news. That's great news. Where is she? Can I talk to her? Can I see her? Over."

"Hold your horses, Kuan Hee. Calm down. She's fine and shipshape. She's been taken to the same ship. Your parents will be together shortly. Over."

"It's a miracle. A real miracle. Mr Walmsley. Over."

"Yes, it is. We try to create miracles in the name of freedom. I'll contact you soon when I get status reports on your father's condition. Over."

"Thank you. Mr Walmsley. Over."

"In the meantime, Kuan Hee. Keep safe. Go into hiding. Do not do anything rash. You understand? Over."

"I understand, sir. I understand. Over."

"Mr Walmsley says I have to hide. We have to hide."

"Can we go back to Jalan Naung?"

"Yes, of course. Let's do it now."

Kuan Hee and Lina took an Uber ride back to Hougang. They alighted along Upper Serangoon Road, just before the start of Jalan Nuang. Then they trod towards his house. It was almost 5:00 a.m. In the silence of the night, they could hear their own footsteps. They were careful not to speak, for in the night, their conversation would appear crystal clear in the bedrooms of their sleeping neighbours. Who knew—one of them could snitch on them!

At the turn into the row of terrace houses next to his house, they paused. There was a car parked outside 79 Jalan Naung. It had a QX licence plate prefix. They could see two heads in the front seat of the car. The G men were looking for them.

"We can't go home right now."

"Where then? My house?"

"Alright. For tonight only."

"It's already morning, dear."

"Mmm."

By the time the pair made it into Lina's bedroom, it was already 5:20 a.m. Lina's mother had woken and left to do her marketing at the shops opposite the road.

The pair slept till late evening. They had been too tired the previous night. They had missed lunch. It was now dinner time. Lina's mother had cooked her favourite dishes today. They tucked into the food ravenously.

In the living room, the television was playing her mother's favourite Korean drama. Suddenly, the programme switched to a news studio and a news presenter appeared on the TV screen. The news bulletin was being broadcast live in English on a Chinese channel.

> This is a special news bulletin. Supreme Leader Tee Bak Chai passed away peacefully at 11:04 a.m. The National Reconciliation Council has appointed his son, Jordan Tee, as the new Supreme Leader. The armed forces have pledged allegiance to the new Supreme Leader whose appointment starts today.
>
> Supreme Leader Tee died of a heart attack. His body will lie in state at Parliament House from tomorrow at 9:00 a.m. till Sunday. A state funeral will be held on Sunday at 2:00 p.m.
>
> All flags will fly at half mast from today till the day of the funeral. The public is advised to wear black or non-bright colours till Sunday. All entertainment programmes are hereby cancelled.
> This concludes the special news bulletin.

The Korean programme was abruptly cancelled and instead sombre music was played the rest of the evening. It was the same on other channels in Singapore.

Kuan Hee and Lina stood glued to the television. They were shocked beyond words.

Is it true that Colonel Tee the dictator has died? they

wondered.

But Jordan had taken over as the Supreme Leader. That meant Colonel Tee had undergone the operation. But the operation was supposed to be this morning and Kuan Hee's father had been rescued early this morning.

"It only means one thing."

"What?"

"Colonel Tee had his operation, not this morning, but most probably yesterday morning. We were too late to prevent him from going ahead with it."

"So Colonel Tee is now Jordan?"

"Yes, dear, I'm afraid so."

"How can this happen? We overheard him saying Thursday."

"Yes, you and I heard it right. He must have got wind of something. He must have gotten suspicious. It could be big Tizzy. He must have realized it was a spying device and changed his schedule."

"So he is going to live! He's not dying after all."

"Yes, I'm afraid so. I'm afraid that's the unfortunate truth."

"We've got to do something or our whole life will be messed up. We won't have our freedom back. We won't be able to get on with our normal lives."

"We've got to meet up with Tim. And Navin. We've got to get their help to deal with this dictator."

"Yes. Yes."

"Lina, why is my Korean programme not showing?" asked Lina's mother. Lina explained to her mother what had happened.

WHATSAPP:
"Meet at usual place. 8:00 p.m. today," texted Lina.
"OK. *Long time no see.* Where have you guys been?" texted Tim.
"It's a long story," texted Lina.

"Where the hell is Kuan Hee?" texted Tim.

"With me," texted Lina.

"Has he changed his phone number?" texted Tim.

"Tell you everything when we meet," texted Lina.

"OK," texted Tim.

"Tim must be pretty angry. He's never used 'hell' on me."

"Can't blame him. We practically disappeared, you know."

The usual place meant ToastBox café in Hougang Mall. The pair got their bags and, after saying goodbye to Lina's mother, went towards the lift.

"Look, there are police cars downstairs."

"Two of them. And there are plainclothes in the car park."

"And over there in the void deck at the opposite block."

"I have a sneaky feeling that they are looking for us. After Dad's escape, they must want me pretty bad. They need me to get Dad back."

"How did they know you are here?"

"Remember the police cameras in the lift lobby? I've always been suspicious of them. Looks like I'm right. The cameras are connected to a central monitoring station." Kuan Hee paused. He was in deep thought.

"They must have used supercomputers to do face recognition scans on all the camera footages in the lifts in Singapore. That's how they found me. They used algorithms. That must be it."

"They haven't come up for us yet."

"They still do not know which unit we are in—unless they do a house-to-house search. Gosh! I think that's what they are going to do soon. We've got to get out of here."

"How? They are downstairs."

"You can see that they have just arrived. We've still got time to make a getaway. Quick! Let's use that staircase."

The pair scrambled down sixteen flights of stairs—Lina lived on the eighth storey. There was a camera monitoring the bottom of this staircase but they had no time to bother about it. They snuck into the car park at the far end, away from the two police cars, and ran towards Upper Serangoon Road. It was a close shave.

"Lina, quick. Call your mother. Tell her to tell these people she has not seen me."

"OK. OK. I will."

"Phew. What a lucky escape."

CHAPTER 23

Tim was getting impatient. He had been sipping his cuppa waiting for Kuan Hee and Lina to turn up, and he had just finished the coffee. There was no sign of the pair. They finally did turn up, after sizing up the surroundings. Boy, did they had an earful from him.

"You guys are some bunch of friends," said Tim as the pair sat down beside him.

"Sorry. Sorry. A thousand apologies," said Kuan Hee.

"We're really sorry, Tim," said Lina.

"First, you disappeared for ages without so much as a word. Now you make me wait for you," said Tim. "What the hell is up with you guys anyway?"

It is the second time he is using this cuss word, thought Lina.

"You two guys, spending many weeks by yourselves, ignoring your best friend, worming into each other's hearts," said Tim.

"Wait a minute. Hold your horses," said Kuan Hee.

Then his voice dropped to a whisper. "Tim, we have got some serious stuff to discuss," he said. "But we can't do it here. Let's drink up and move somewhere else quieter."

The ToastBox cafe in Hougang Mall was only meant to

be a meeting point.

Hougang MRT Station was not a quiet station today. There were strange looking men, either standing or sitting on the benches next to the station, poring over the faces of people who entered the station. They had to be looking for Kuan Hee.

The three friends abandoned their plan to travel on the MRT. Instead, they took an Uber ride to Punggol Park, on the outskirts of Hougang town. They sat next to some swings on the playground. It was deserted.

Kuan Hee proceeded to tell Tim what had happened to him and his family the past few weeks. He ended with a blow-by-blow account of the commandoes' rescue mission in Maju Camp.

"Fancy going on an adventure of a lifetime without me," said Tim.

"No, it wasn't an adventure. It was dangerous. It was nerve-racking, you know," said Lina.

"Funny. There's nothing in the news about the attack on Maju Camp," said Tim.

"Yes, strange that it wasn't reported on," said Kuan Hee. "An attack by unknown military force not getting into the news is indeed strange."

"And it is true—Jordan is no longer the Jordan we know. He's become his father," said Tim.

"Yes. And my Dad was held in detention because Colonel Tee wanted him to do the operation for him and his son."

"So that's why Jordan went missing the day he was supposed to lead the protest in Orchard Road," said Tim.

"That's right. I had asked Jordan when he came to my house one night to seek shelter," said Kuan Hee. "He was in fear, but he wouldn't reveal what was happening—no matter how hard I tried to pry it out of him."

"Now he's become his father—the new dictator of Singapore," said Lina.

"Is that why you are on the run now?" said Tim.

"I have no choice. Colonel Tee or Jordan—whoever's in charge now wants to get my Dad through me," said Kuan Hee.

"What can we do?" asked Tim.

"That's the reason we are here—to discuss how to deal with Colonel Tee or Jordan," said Kuan Hee.

"We need weapons," said Tim, "if we are going against him or them."

"Yes. We need a plan too," said Kuan Hee. "I have a proposal."

"Out with it man," said Tim.

"I want to try to take him out on the day of the funeral," said Kuan Hee.

"How?" said Lina.

"As he—I mean Jordan follows the coffin, I intend to take a shot at him," said Kuan Hee.

"You want to kill Jordan?" said Lina.

"For goodness's sake, Lina. It's not Jordan now. Jordan's dead. It's Colonel Tee in Jordan's body. He's evil all over. If we don't kill him, he will continue to harm people. Singapore will not be safe from his clutches."

"I've got friends in the army. They are in national service but they work in the armory," said Tim.

"Good. We need some SAR21s," said Kuan Hee. "Also, try to get me a Steyr SSG 69."

"We've also got artillery. AleXander are our artillery," said Lina.

"But, they are too small to be of any use," said Tim.

"No. They are not. Alex has got laser weapons and Xander can launch rockets," said Lina.

"Calling Kuan Hee. Calling Kuan Hee. Over."

"It's the Brigadier," said Kuan Hee. He pulled out the walkie-talkie from his backpack.

"This is Kuan Hee. Over."

"Kuan Hee. I see they haven't caught you yet. Over."

"Mr Walmsley. You seem to be hinting they should catch me. Over."

"Kuan Hee. Just joking. Over."

"Me too, Mr Walmsley. I was just joking. Over."

"I am calling because I need to wrap up our operations. Over."

"What do you mean, Mr Walmsley? Over."

"It means—I need to get you out of the country—to safety. Over."

"Be with my parents? Over."

"Yes, Kuan Hee. Let you reunite with your parents. Isn't that great? Over."

"I'd love to join my parents. But I also need to tie up some loose ends here. Over."

"What exactly are you talking about? Over."

"I want to kill the dictator. Over."

"Don't be rash. Kuan Hee. You can't possibly do it alone. Just come with us to safety. Don't let your parents worry about you. Over."

"Are you going to join your parents?" asked Lina.

"You heard me right? I told him I am staying put. I'm going to kill Jordan Tee if it is the last thing I get to do," said Kuan Hee. "Don't try to dissuade me. I've made up my mind."

"Where are you staying now?" asked Tim.

"That is what I want to talk to you about," said Kuan Hee. "I can't put up at Lina's place anymore. The plainclothes are swarming over her place, looking for me there."

"So you want me to put you up. Is that it?" said Tim.

"Yeah. We're good friends, right? Buddies right?" said Kuan Hee.

"Yeah, but—" said Tim.

"No buts. Just do it," said Kuan Hee.

"I can't take you to my house. That's for sure," said Tim. "But—you can hide in the storeroom above my grandfather's shop."

"The one in Upper Serangoon Road—Ah Kong Reflexology Centre?" said Kuan Hee.

"That's the one," said Tim.

"That's a good idea," said Lina approvingly.

"So when can I move in?" asked Kuan Hee.

"You mean—we," said Lina.

"Both of you are staying?" said Tim.

"Appears so, Tim," said Kuan Hee.

"Let me ask my grandfather first," said Tim. "Give me a minute." Tim drew out his smartphone and tapped a button on it. Then he rattled off in *Hock Chew*. Being not conversant with the dialect, Kuan Hee and Lina didn't understand a single word.

"OK. Set. My grandfather's agreed," said Tim. "Shall we go there now?"

"Yes, let's," echoed the pair.

CHAPTER 24

Ah Kong Reflexology Centre was a foot massage shop in the middle of a row of three-storey shop houses along Upper Serangoon Road. Access to the upper floors was via a concrete staircase that ran the entire width of the shop. The staircase was situated outside the shop—on one side. As the three friends approached the shop, the pungent smell of liniments and Chinese herbs permeated the air.

"*Ah Kong*," all greeted in unison.

Tim's grandfather waved to them, said something to Tim and the threesome climbed the stairs. Tim had gotten a key to the second-storey premises from him. They found themselves in a wide corridor with two rooms on both ends and an open area in the centre. The toilet was in the rear. Tim opened the door on their right. The room was about the size of a HDB master-bedroom. He opened the glass-paneled windows to reveal the road below. Downstairs, on the roadside, were parked vehicles. Some cars were double-parked. It was a popular waiting area for vehicles, for a dozen food shops straddled the road. It was almost a dining paradise.

"Here's where you will be staying. No air-conditioning, I'm afraid. Only this table fan," said Tim. "The other room is a storeroom."

"It's a super place. No need for air-conditioning. The fan's great," said Kuan Hee. He placed his backpack on the small table at one wall.

"There's no bed," said Lina.

"No need for a bed. We can get a mat and some blankets from the shops later," said Kuan Hee.

"Sorry. This place isn't meant to be a bedroom," said Tim. "It is actually a spare storeroom."

"It's alright. We should be the ones saying sorry—for putting you out like this," said Kuan Hee.

"Let's get cracking," said Tim.

Tim got down to contacting his army mates while Kuan Hee phoned his friends in the students' union.

The spare storeroom above the shop was also the group's meeting venue. It took them two days to put together a workable plan to take down Supreme Leader Jordan Tee. In the meantime, Tim's army buddies had handed him the weapons he needed. These were laid out on the table in front of them.

"SAR21s," said Kuan Hee.

"Check. Three SAR21s," said Tim, "with a hundred cartridges."

"Steyr SSG 69," said Kuan Hee.

"Check. One Steyr SSG 69," said Tim, "with two magazines—each with five cartridges."

"Wah. It's so easy to get these weapons," said Lina.

"These are not from the active armories, so they won't be missed. These come from a five-year reserve stock," said Tim.

"What's that?" asked Lina.

"This is stuff kept in deep freeze—opened only in times of war," said Tim. "Too many of them stacked together in the warehouse. Nobody will miss a thing."

"I didn't know the Singapore army keeps such a large supply of weapons," said Lina. "These weapons must surely need many warehouses."

"The Singapore army not only has reserve weapons; it also has reserve tanks, armored personnel carriers, three-tonners and so on and so forth," said Tim.

"By George, where do they keep them?" asked Lina.

"Oh. That's a trade secret," said Tim, amused.

"We have to find bags long enough to fit these weapons," said Lina.

"No need, Lina. They can be taken apart and reassembled," said Tim. "They will fit in a backpack."

"Gosh. You guys are really cool," said Lina. "Fancy knowing how to handle these rifles."

"We didn't spend two years doing national service in the army for fun, you know," said Navin, chuckling as he ran his fingers over the SAR21 in his hands.

"Did you manage to get some grenades?" said Kuan Hee.

"Eh. That one—quite difficult to get our hands on," said Tim. "No luck."

"Never mind. What we have are good enough," said Kuan Hee. "We also have AeXander's rockets and laser weapon system."

"Did you manage to rope in Navin?" said Lina.

"Yeah. He's in on the plan," said Kuan Hee. He will join us tonight. We're all sleeping here tonight. Just in case."

"Don't you need to practice using the Steyr SSG 69?" said Lina.

"Lina, he doesn't. He went to sniper school during NS. He's unlike the rest of us army guys—he's a sharpshooter through and through," said Tim.

"I'm not that good," said Kuan Hee, blushing.

"He is—the best of the crop, Lina," said Tim.

"I believe you, Tim. I believe you," said Lina. Kuan Hee was always modest with his achievements.

"We'll wait for Navin to come before we go through tomorrow's mission," said Kuan Hee.

It was 9:00 p.m. when Kuan Hee, Lina and Tim finished their dinner. Navin had just arrived and they were now seated on the floor in the room. There was a long silence. Then Navin tuned in to an Internet radio station on his smartphone and pop music flooded the room.

"So everyone understands the high risks in tomorrow's operation," said Kuan Hee. All nodded.

"You can choose to back out now, if you wish to," said Kuan Hee. No one said a word.

"Navin, OK?" said Kuan Hee. "Your girlfriend?"

"OK. I didn't tell her a thing," said Navin.

"Tim? OK?" said Kuan Hee. Tim didn't have a girlfriend.

"Lina. You stay in the background—at this spot," said Kuan Hee, pointing to a spot on the map in front of them. "If anything goes awry, run and then hide. Do not turn back. Do not come to us—even if we are injured or—dead."

Lina was hesitant. Her lips were quivering. A moment ago she was nonchalant about the danger they were getting themselves into.

"Lina, do you understand?" said Kuan Hee.

"Eh. Yes," said Lina.

Kuan Hee went through their mission, detailing the positions each would take the next day. He got the rest to repeat what he had said. His national service stint was coming into good use.

"No one leaves this place from now on," said Kuan Hee. All nodded. "Tomorrow, we will take down the dictator." All nodded again.

"Our rendezvous is at Punggol Park after the mission, whether sunshine or rain," said Kuan Hee. Sunshine and rain were codes for success and failure respectively.

There were three guys and four rifles so one SAR21 was a spare which they would take with them—just in case. Then Kuan Hee, Navin and Tim cleaned their weapons. They let Lina try cleaning the spare SAR21.

The hours ticked away. Dawn was breaking but the mission members had not slept a wink. They lay resting against the wall, staring into space. No doubt, everyone was tense and uneasy.

What will tomorrow bring? they were wondering.

Navin was fingering a cigarette. He was the only smoker among the four friends.

"When Jordan falls—will another dictator take his place?" said Navin.

"I don't know. I really don't know," said Kuan Hee. He was right. The politics of a country was unpredictable. Just when you thought everything was going fine, someone might drop a bomb in your midst.

"We'll take one step at a time," said Tim.

"Yeah. Cross the bridge when we come to it," said Lina.

CHAPTER 25

The area around Parliament Building in North Bridge Road had been cordoned off. Armored personnel carriers guarded the junctions of High Street and Parliament Place. Soldiers formed a chain across these roads. There were spectators behind them, and along both sides of North Bridge Road. These people had come to bade farewell to the late Supreme Leader Colonel Tee, albeit involuntarily for most of them.

The mission members were across Elgin Bridge, in the crowd lining South Bridge Road. Security was not tight in this area; they could slip in unnoticed with their weapons. Navin and Tim's role was to fire at the soldiers and plainclothes after Kuan Hee had done his work. This would give some precious minutes for Kuan Hee to make his getaway. Lina was with the two men. Her job was to keep the spare SAR21 in her backpack. It was needed in case a rifle jammed. She had also been taught how to fire the SAR21 should the need arise.

Kuan Hee had taken up position on a staircase landing in an apartment building across the river. His target was within the effective range of the Steyr SSG 69 which was eight hundred metres. He had a clear line of sight of this part of North Bridge Road where the funeral procession would be moving through. There were army snipers at some buildings; the glint of light on their scopes gave away their positions. He made sure he was out of their sight.

The cortege of mourners was coming out of the front gate of Parliament House. As the procession turned into the main road, a convoy of vehicles—two Mercedes limousines and four Volvos joined the group of people surrounding the new Supreme Leader. Men were standing on both sides of the first two Volvos, holding on to opened doors. There had to be scores of these plainclothes mingling with the procession. The Supreme Leader, with his mother next to him, was flanked by his bodyguards.

Kuan Hee loaded the magazine and readied the rifle. The magazine held five rounds. He could take five shots without having to reload. His sweaty hands slid slightly on the smooth molded fiberglass. He grabbed the frame firmly. Then he cocked the Steyr SSG 69 and pressed his eye against the scope. The new Supreme Leader had come into its cross-hairs. He took a deep breath and held it. Then he squeezed the trigger. A shot rang out and, in the distance, there was a cry. Then pandemonium set in. Bodyguards were clambering over the new Supreme Leader and bundling him into the nearby Mercedes.

Have I hit him? wondered Kuan Hee.

He wasn't sure. He didn't get to make a second shot, for some army snipers were now targeting his position. A few bullets whizzed through the air. Some hit the wall, two ricocheted off the wall, with one landing in his left shoulder. It was piercing pain that hit him. Kuan Hee knew he had to leave fast. He slung the rifle on one shoulder and clambered down the stairs to the ground floor. It was now his team members' job to keep the soldiers and plainclothes busy so that he could make his getaway safely.

Lina was at the bottom of the stairs waiting for him. She had been worried and, despite his order, had run to the apartment building to look for him. She was in a frenzy when she spotted him. But she recovered from shock in time to help stop the bleeding from his wound with a packet of tissue paper. Both swaggered towards New Bridge Road. They stopped along the way for a few seconds so he could dismantle the rifle and put it in his backpack.

At the chaotic scene, Navin and Tim fired at the soldiers and plainclothes. People were running in all directions. The duo were careful not to shoot into the crowd. Then they ran into a row of shop houses and turned into the streets of Chinatown. Hovering in the air were two drones. Navin shot them down easily, for he was a marksman in his NS days. Then they dismantled their rifles and mingled with the crowd. As planned, Navin and Tim separated in Hong Kong Street. They would meet at Punggol Park.

Lina and Kuan Hee had not counted on him being injured. With his injury, there was no way he could move through crowded Singapore without being spotted. Lina phoned her eldest brother for help. The pair took cover in the staircase of an old shop house.

Her brother arrived in his van within fifteen minutes—he had been on an errand for his company—buying cartons of toilet paper. He hid the pair under bags of toilet paper and drove off. He drove along Merchant Road towards Clemenceau Avenue. There was a road block being prepared at the junction ahead. Soldiers were hastily getting metal barricades off a three-tonner. A soldier raised his hand to signal to Lina's brother to stop the vehicle. The soldier was disarmed by her brother's co-operative gesture—he had volunteered to unload the cargo onto the road for the soldier to inspect the van. He waved the van off.

The van raced through the city area and entered the suburban districts. Then it cruised into Hougang. Lina's brother stopped the van in the car park of Punggol Park.

Then he opened the door and jumped in.

"The coast is clear," said Lina's brother. "You can come out now."

Lina and Kuan Hee pushed aside the bags of toilet paper. Her hands were coated with blood, so were her blouse and shorts. Luckily, she managed to stop the bleeding. Kuan Hee was feeling faint. He was in pain.

There was no sign of Tim or Navin. Hopefully they had managed to escape. She couldn't phone them. They had agreed not to use their smartphones for fear their calls were being monitored.

"He needs medical attention urgently. We can't wait for your friends," said Lina's brother.

"Where shall we go? said Lina. "Kuan Hee, what shall I do?" But Kuan Hee was delirious and could not hear her.

"Let's take him to Dr Koh. He won't tell on us," said Lina's brother. Dr Koh had been the Goh family's go-to doctor for many years. He ran a clinic in Hougang Avenue Five.

"OK. Let's move, then," said Lina.

Her brother drove them to Hougang Avenue Five. He left them in the van and strode to the clinic to speak to the doctor. Then he returned to take the pair into the clinic through the back door. The clinic had already closed for business but the doctor was still in. The doctor had shooed off his clinic assistant before opening the back door for the sudden visitors.

"The bullet is lodged in the flesh. Luckily, it's not pierced any organs. Landed away from the heart and missed the clavicle—the collar bone—by almost a centimetre. Lucky chap," said Dr Koh. "I'll have to pry it out."

He took a pair of forceps and some gauze to clean the wound. Then he injected an anesthetic into the skin around the wound. He waited for a minute for the anesthetic to take effect and proceeded to remove the bullet from the shoulder with another pair of forceps.

Kuan Hee was feverish and incoherent.

"He'll be fine. No major damage done," said Dr Koh. "I'll give him some antibiotics to kill the germs."

"Doctor, he is still running a fever. What shall I do?" said Lina.

"I've given him an antipyretic injection. The fever will subside within hours. In the meantime, you'll need to monitor his condition. Let him take the paracetamol as prescribed. If his condition worsens, you can call me."

"Thank you, doctor," said Lina.

"Here's the bullet. It seems different from bullets I have seen," said Dr Koh. "Dispose of it where no one can find—he's a brave lad, fighting the dictatorship. Not many fine youngsters like him nowadays."

"Thank you for saving his life, doctor," said Lina.

"No problem. It's my duty to save people," said Dr Koh. "Just be careful with him for the next few days. Remember—no seafood for a week."

"I'll. I'll. Bye Dr Koh," said Lina.

Dr Koh switched off the lights in the clinic. He did not want to draw attention. He opened the back door, glanced around and then waved them to the door. He watched them getting into the van before closing the door.

"Where to now?" asked Lina's brother. She directed him to Ah Kong's shop in Upper Serangoon. It was late evening and darkness was setting in. Her brother waited till the walkway was clear of people before carrying Kuan Hee up into the second-storey premises. Then he left.

Lina did not switch on the lights; there was ambient light from the road outside filtering into the room through the windows. There they were—Kuan Hee lying motionless on a mat and she sitting next to him, fingering his hair. She would look at the bundle of bloodied clothes in the supermarket bag across from them. Then she would look at Kuan Hee. Occasionally, she would wipe off her tears and then with the same wet fingers, she would pat his hair. When she undertook to join the mission, Kuan Hee had told her that injury was a foreseeable result, but she had not counted on it actually happening—not to her beloved Kuan Hee. She was in a bind. Not knowing what to do next, she thought the best thing was to do nothing but wait—wait for Kuan Hee to wake up, wait for Tim and Navin to return. She hoped they were alright.

It was 1:00 a.m. Lina heard some sounds coming from the corridor. First, it was a door creaking open. Then, it was the patter of footsteps. She froze. She held Kuan Hee close to her.

What am I to do now? she wondered.

The door opened and who did she see standing there?—Navin and Tim!

"I'm so glad to see both of you," said Lina. She was now tearing.

"How's he?" asked Navin.

"His fever is going down. The doctor has given him some fever medicine." Then she told the two men what had happened in their absence.

"He's indeed lucky. He escaped death," said Navin. He related how Tim and he made their escape. When they reached the rendezvous place, there was no sign of the pair. They waited in vain for hours. They thought something bad had happened to the pair. Then they decided to return to the shop, hoping against hope that the pair would be there.

"It's good both of you are safe," said Navin.

"We need to hide the weapons," said Tim. "It's too dangerous to keep them here. There are workers coming up and down regularly for the goods on the second level."

"Let's bury them," said Navin.

"It's a good idea," said Tim. "I'll think of a place."

"Aren't you going to return them to your army friends?" asked Lina.

"We may need them later," said Tim. "Besides, the weapons won't be missed for months. And if we can end the dictatorship, my army friends won't get into trouble."

"Any news on the Supreme Leader?" asked Lina. "I've been too busy taking care of Kuan Hee to do anything else."

"It appears he wasn't injured. Someone behind him took the bullet for him," said Navin. "That's what the news said."

"I don't trust the news. It's all propaganda," said Tim. "The only way to be sure he is unharmed is to see him on live television."

"We went to so much trouble," said Lina, "and Kuan Hee got hurt badly as a result—and this guy—nothing has happened to this guy?"

There was silence in the dark room.

"Lina, look. There are pictures of you and Kuan Hee on channelsingapore.com. You are wanted by the military government," said Navin.

"These shots were taken yesterday," said Tim. "The cameras must have caught you leaving the apartment building."

Lina looked at the news article, then at her two friends. She was sullen.

"They are bound to identify me. What if they go after my mother—and my brothers?" said Lina in despair.

Navin and Tim had no answer.

Kuan Hee, Kuan Hee, if you could only wake up and tell me what to do, she thought. But Kuan Hee had not heard her thoughts. He was asleep.

CHAPTER 26

Early next morning, Navin and Tim left in a car that Navin had borrowed from his brother. They had taken the weapons and ammunition with them. Kuan Hee was still asleep. There were many thoughts running through Lina's mind; she had not slept the whole night.

"Calling Kuan Hee. Calling Kuan Hee. Over."

It was the Brigadier on the walkie-talkie. Lina got out the walkie talkie from the backpack. She pressed the PTT button.

"Yes, Brigadier Walmsley. This is Lina. Eh. Over."

"Oh it's you, Lina. Where is Kuan Hee? I need to talk to him. Over."

"Kuan Hee—he's—he's unconscious. He was shot in his shoulder. Over."

There was a moment of silence.

"I see. Is he the one who attempted to assassinate the Supreme Leader? Over."

"Yes. He, me, and some friends of ours. But he's the only one injured. Over."

"Is his condition serious? Have you sought medical attention? Over."

"His fever has subsided, but he hasn't woken yet. A

doctor removed the bullet from his shoulder. He said he'll be fine—only a flesh wound. Over."

There was silence over the airwaves again.

"I see. Lina, when he wakes up, can you tell him his father's in stable condition. He is now conscious. He wants to talk to Kuan Hee. Over."

"He's conscious now? That's great news. I'll tell Kuan Hee. I'll ask him to call you. Over." Lina was beaming. She had forgotten her woes—for the moment.

"And, Lina. If his condition becomes worse—call me. Over."

"I'll, Brigadier Walmsley. Over."

"Keep safe. Don't do rash things. Bye for now. Over."

"Bye bye, Brigadier Walmsley. Over."

Lina put down the transceiver. She flashed a weak smile.

Kuan Hee will be so happy to learn his father is awake and in stable condition, Lina thought.

"Kuan Hee, when are you going to wake up? I'm all alone. I'm afraid." He did not answer her.

Navin had told her to turn off her smartphone. The G men could be tracking signals from her smartphone. She remembered Kuan Hee's iPhone was powered by the Polaris satellite. She used his iPhone to surf the Websites. She was looking for news of the assassination and their wanted status.

On the Ministry of Homeland Security's Website, there were grainy pictures of her and Kuan Hee. There were no names mentioned—only pictures. Perhaps, the G had not been able to identify them positively. Perhaps, it was hoping people would recognize them and feed information to the G.

There were no reports on Navin and Tim. The G had not got wind of them yet.

At least, things are not that bad, Lina told herself.

It was midmorning when Kuan Hee stirred. Lina

opened her eyes. She had felt him touch her arm. Kuan Hee had woken.

"Where am I?" He had opened his eyes and was now looking around the room. Then he remembered where he was. "Lina, your eyes are red."

"Thank God you are awake. I was so worried."

Kuan Hee by now was conscious of his surroundings and of the situation they were in.

He pressed two fingers on his eyebrows. "Have Navin and Tim got away safely?"

"Yes, dear. They are safe and well. They've gone to hide the weapons."

"You look thin. Have you eaten?" He looked around again. There were some buns on the table.

"Tim bought some buns from a bakery. But I wasn't hungry. Kuan Hee, we are now fugitives. Our pictures are everywhere on the news Websites."

"It's alright, Lina. We can handle it. Just need to be more careful."

"And Kuan Hee, the Brigadier called this morning. Your father—he's conscious and in stable condition."

Kuan Hee's pale face lit up.

"He is? What else did Mr Walmsley say?"

"He wants you to call him."

"Quick, pass me the walkie-talkie."

Lina handed him the walkie-talkie.

"Calling Mr Walmsley. This is Kuan Hee. Calling Mr Walmsley. Over."

"Hi. Kuan Hee. You are awake. Over."

"Mr Walmsley. My father—he's OK? Really OK? Over."

"Yes, Kuan Hee. Alive and kicking. Do you want to talk to him? Over."

"Yes, Mr Walmsley, Of course. When? How? Over."

"In fact, he's right here now—next to me. I'm on the ship with him. Let me pass the walkie-talkie to him. Eh. Professor Wang, your son. Kuan Hee wants to speak with you … Kuan Hee, Kuan Hee. It's Dad. Are you alright, son? Over."

"Yes, Dad. Great to hear your voice again. How are you and Mum? Over."

"We're fine, son. Say hallo to your mum. Over."

"Hi. Mum. Miss you guys. Over."

"Hi. Kuan Hee. Your Dad is fine. He can walk now. I'm worried about you. Is your shoulder better? Over."

"Mum and Dad. I am OK. Really miss you guys. Over." Kuan Hee was at a loss for words. The Wang family was reunited again—albeit over the airwaves.

Soon we'll be together, soon, thought Kuan Hee.

"Son, I have an important thing to tell you. Listen carefully. Over."

"Yes Dad. I'm all ears. Go ahead. Over."

"Kuan Hee. You know I operated on Colonel Tee's mind. Colonel Tee's memories are now embedded in his son, Jordan's mind. Over."

"Yes, Dad. I know. Over."

"Now, here's the important part. I deliberately created a schizophrenic condition during the memory transfer process. So now, Colonel Tee does not control Jordan's mind completely. At times, Jordan's memories will overlap with his memories. I did not erase Jordan's memories completely. Do you understand me so far, son? Eh. Over."

"Yes, Dad. You mean Colonel Tee is now like Dr Jekyll and Mr Hyde in Robert Louis Stevenson's novel? Over."

"Correct, son. I purposely created a Jekyll and Hyde condition in their memories. Over."

"Dad, what can Jordan do? He's powerless. Over."

"But, you see, son. His men do not know he's Jordan. You and I know. That's the difference. Over."

"I understand. Dad. How do I wake up Jordan? How do I know when Jordan is in control? Over."

"Now that's a problem. Actually, I couldn't find a way to activate Jordan's memories. Otherwise, it would have been plain sailing—just switch over to Jordan permanently and everything is OK again in the country. The only way is to observe them. See when they are Jordan and when they are Colonel Tee. Use the housefly and the dragonfly. Over."

"OK, Dad. I understand. Over."

"Son, now we have a way to deal with Colonel Tee. Listen. When Colonel Tee acts like Jordan—when he talks like Jordan, persuade him to undo the harm his father has done to the country. Over."

"How? Dad. Over."

"Son. Difficult as it is—You are going to have to ask Jordan to kill himself. Save the country by killing himself. Over."

There was silence. Kuan Hee was shocked by his father's words.

"Kuan Hee. Listen. You have to do it. That's the only way to rid Singapore of this menace. Over."

There was no response from Kuan Hee again.

"Kuan Hee. Listen again. If this is difficult to do. Find another way. Use their Jekyll and Hyde condition to deal with Colonel Tee. Over."

"OK, Dad. I will think over what you have said. Over."

"You heard what my Dad said, right?" said Kuan Hee. "What shall I do?" Kuan Hee had indeed forgotten he had told himself Jordan was now no longer the Jordan they knew.

Minutes later, Kuan Hee spoke again.

"Another way—my Dad mentioned, another way. I need to think over this other way." Lina left him to his thoughts. When Kuan Hee behaved like this, it would be hours before he spoke to her—or any one else. It was typical Kuan Hee syndrome. He was having a recurring attack now. Suddenly, she felt hungry. She devoured the buns on the table.

"Lina, I'm famished. Let's get something to eat." It was

2:30 p.m. and Kuan Hee had finished with his thoughts and his stomach was growling. But Lina had cleaned the table of the buns.

"We can't go out yet. It's not safe. Let's wait a little longer. Navin and Tim should be back soon."

"Let's not wait. I'm really hungry; I could eat a horse."

"But you haven't fully recovered. You still look pale."

There was just no dissuading Kuan Hee when he had made up his mind.

CHAPTER 27

Kuan Hee and Lina were now fugitives. There were pictures of them, albeit grainy ones, flashed across five-metre tall screens mounted at vantage points on buildings and at traffic light junctions. These screens, a common fixture across the island, served advertisements and government notices.

The pair were just across the road from Kovan Heartland Mall when they saw their faces on the large screens. The G notice accompanying their pictures had this statement:

Wanted!
Reward offered for information leading to
the identification and arrest of the
following persons:

The pair instantly recognized themselves. But it would take a discerning eye to pick them out from the throng of people in the streets. And both were now wearing baseball caps. They would have worn face masks if they could but in this day and age, face masks were banned. It had been banned in many countries around the world since the early

2020s.

Soon the pair were at McDonald's, located at the other end of the Kovan Neighbourhood Centre.

"I didn't get your favourite Quarter Pounder for you. I thought Filet-O-Fish would be better—till you fully recover."

They were indeed hungry. Both wolfed down their food. Their next stop was to be NEX Shopping Mall. They wanted to buy some clothes to replace the ones which were soiled with blood. It was crazy; these two were travelling around when the military government was looking for them. Weren't they afraid? In fact, Kuan Hee was trying to lift Lina's spirits. She had been cooped up for ages, and it would do her a world of good to move around—do the things they usually did together. She would feel better, he had hoped. She sorely needed the change.

The pair had come out of the train at Serangoon MRT Station and were moving up the escalator, heading for the exit point. It was then that some police officers of the Transport Command on the lower platform took notice of them and started climbing the same escalator. They were going after them.

Kuan Hee saw them behind the pair and motioned to Lina to run up the final few steps of the escalator. Instead of heading for the exit point, they turned into the passageway leading to the Circle Line. They ran onto a long travelator, brushed past other commuters and strode towards the other end of the travelator. The policemen were hot on their heels.

They ran down another escalator to the lower platform of the Circle Line's Serangoon Station. The train was unloading passengers at this station and the pair dashed in just in time, for the doors were closing onto Kuan Hee's backpack. The first few of the policemen were too late. They could only watch the train with the pair inside ramble off. Kuan Hee took a deep breath and held his injured shoulder. The pain had returned. He had overexerted himself, but he told Lina he was all right.

At the next station, the pair got off and waited for the next train moving in the opposite direction. They were heading back to Serangoon. Kuan Hee had said other policemen could be lying in wait for them at the next few stations. The train came in two minutes and the pair went in. They were careful to keep their faces away from the overhead cameras on the train. This train stopped at Serangoon Station, where minutes earlier they had boarded another train. They got off at this station and walked back to the North-East Line's Serangoon Station. This time they blended with the crowd of passengers heading in the same direction.

On the platform of North-East Line's Serangoon Station, the pair boarded a train heading towards Harbourfront. They thought they had shaken off their pursuers. But they were wrong. At Dhoby Ghaut Interchange, there were policemen piling onto the platform. Evidently they had got wind of the pair's movement. They were waiting for the train to come to a stop. Their eyes were on the passengers on the train. Kuan Hee and Lina were trapped. It would be difficult for them to escape. Luckily, the train cars were teeming with passengers for Dhoby Ghaut Interchange was a busy station. The pair squeezed through the packed platform, hunching their backs and making sure they were in the thick of the crowd of passengers.

But lady luck was against them this time. They thought they were clever, but they had forgotten their caps were a giveaway. An eagle-eyed policeman had spotted their caps and signaled to the others the pair's position. Then all hell broke loose as the policemen congregated near the escalator which the pair were about to board. The crowd was terrified for policemen were running into them. Two policemen elbowed their way into the crowd and grabbed hold of Kuan Hee. They couldn't reach Lina, for she had followed the other passengers up the long escalator to the ground level. It was too late for Kuan Hee. He had been caught. Lina made a getaway when she reached the entrance of the station. Soon she was out of sight of the station. She sat sobbing at a corner of a building, oblivious to the curious stares of passers-by.

Kuan Hee was bundled into a van and taken to the Police Cantonment Complex in New Bridge Road. His personal belongings and belt were taken from him and placed in a big envelope which had his name written on it. Then he was taken to a holding cell of the Warrant Enforcement Unit. It was slightly bigger than an HDB living room. The floor was concrete screed. At the opposite end of the cell door was a squat pan with a low concrete wall next to it, presumably to afford some privacy to the squat pan user. Except for this, the room was bare. There were three other male occupants in the cell.

No one said a word to him in the first two hours he spent in the cell. He was not told why they were holding him. Nor was he charged with a crime.

Then a policeman came for him. He was handcuffed and taken upstairs to a room on the third level. It seemed to be an interview room. There was a video camera standing on one side of the room. A table and two chairs were the only other furniture in the room. The policeman handcuffed him to a chair and left the room.

It was cold in the room. It was to be another half hour before the door opened and two policemen walked in. One had three pips on his epaulette—a Senior Inspector. The other had a crest and two pips—a Superintendent.

The Superintendent sat opposite Kuan Hee. He took out an Identification Card from an envelope and placed it on the table.

"You must be Wang Kuan Hee."

"Yes. I am him, sir."

"Do you know why you are here?"

"No, sir."

"Let me tell you."

The Superintendent took out a large photograph from the envelope and placed it in front of Kuan Hee. It was a grainy picture of Kuan Hee in a lift lobby.

"Does this face ring a bell?"

"Yes, sir. He looks like me."

"Yes, indeed. Do you know who he is?"

"No, sir."

"Let me tell you then. He is a suspected killer."

"Killer, sir? Whom did he kill?"

"Oh. My mistake. He did not kill anyone. He attempted to kill the Supreme Leader of the NRC."

"He is that brave? Fancy having the guts to kill the Prime Minister of the country."

"Yes. He sure is brave. He had the guts, as you have said, to kill a VIP of the country. An ordinary person would not dare to do such a thing. In fact, many brave souls in this country also do not have the courage to carry out an assassination on this VIP."

"I am not him, sir."

"You do not look like a brave chap, I must say."

"Of course, sir. I am timid. I am *kiasi*. I will never be able to summon the courage to kill a person."

"Assuming you were this guy—why would you want to risk your life doing such a dangerous thing?"

"For life, liberty and the pursuit of happiness, of course."

"Well said. Very well said."

The Superintendent clenched his fists and paused for some minutes.

"Kumar."

"Yes, sir."

"Take him away. Return his things. Set him free."

"Sir? This man is a highly wanted criminal."

"Wanted by whom, Kumar?"

"Wanted by the military government, of course."

"So are we the military, Kumar?"

"No, sir, but we report to them, sir."

"We don't report to them. We report to the Commissioner of Police. And he is in their custody. So we report to no one now. Do you understand?"

"Yes, sir. I understand, sir."

"Kumar—do as you are told."

"Yes, sir."

"And Kumar—don't tell a soul."

"Sir, how do I report this?"

"Do you need me to tell you exactly what you need to do?"

"Yes, sir. I mean, no, sir."

"Kumar, report this as a case of mistaken identity."

"Yes, sir. I will do as ordered, sir."

Turning to Kuan Hee, the Superintendent nodded and left the room.

CHAPTER 28

It was a tired Kuan Hee who climbed the stairs to the storeroom above Ah Kong Reflexology Centre. He had no way to contact Lina, for she could not use her smartphone. He thought she had to be here—there was nowhere else for her to go. She could not go home.

As he opened the door, he saw, in the dark room, a figure curled up in a corner, sobbing away. Outside, the traffic droned and the buses rumbled.

He reached for the figure, grasped it with his arms and sobbed in unison with it.

"Kuan Hee. I am scared."

"Me too. Me too."

"Don't leave me. Don't ever leave me, Kuan Hee."

"I won't. I won't."

"Promise me, promise me."

That said, she held him in her bosom. In the darkness, the pair felt their emptiness spread thin and vanish. In its place now was the warmth of their hearts. In each other, they had found home.

"Kuan Hee, I—I want."

She needn't wait long this time. He had glided out of his clothes and was helping her take off hers.

She pushed him into her warm home.

"In there, you're safe. With you, I am safe."

"Mmm."

"Kuan Hee."

"What?"

"I don't want to get pregnant."

"I'll use a condom."

"I don't want a condom. No feeling."

"*Alamak!* What do you want?"

"I want you."

"Alright. I know what to do. Trust me."

The next morning, Navin and Tim finally turned up at the storeroom.

"Where have you been?" asked Kuan Hee.

"You guys went missing for days," said Lina.

"It's a long story," said Tim.

"We kept waiting for you guys," said Lina. "We thought you would be back by noon that day."

"The situation was getting dire. There were road blocks everywhere. Instead of coming here, we went home," said Tim. "We thought if we stayed together, everyone would be caught together. If we were in different places, there is still a chance of survival for some of us."

"The army and the police are swarming the island looking for the people behind the assassination attempt," said Navin. "Every which way we went, there were soldiers and roadblocks."

"I know," said Kuan Hee. "I got caught in the MRT station."

"You did?" said Navin. "You are damned lucky then. You are still here—safe and sound."

"How did you get free?" said Tim. "Did you escape?"

"No, *lah*," said Kuan Hee. "They let me go."

"They let you go?" said Navin. "Just like that? Did they follow you here? Perhaps, it's just a ruse—they want to catch us all in one fell swoop."

"Yeah, I agree," said Tim. He was suddenly a bundle of nerves. "What if they are waiting for us outside? Oh God. My grandfather—they will shut this place for good."

"Calm down, everyone," said Kuan Hee. "Sit down. All of you. Keep away from the window."

It took some minutes before the group of friends collected themselves and the uneasiness subsided.

"My guess—is that the police are not keen on catching us," said Kuan Hee. "The Superintendent who interviewed me said something about the Police Commissioner being held in detention by the army. When he came to this part, he sounded defiant. It was as if he was sore about the matter. And he gave me a strange look when he left the room."

"What strange look is that?" asked Navin.

"I can't put my finger on it," said Kuan Hee. "He nodded to me—as if approving my actions. But he didn't say a word—not a single word."

"That's really strange," said Navin.

"Calling Kuan Hee. This is James Walmsley. Over."

Kuan Hee reached for the walkie-talkie in his backpack.

"Yes, Mr Walmsley. This is Kuan Hee speaking. Over."

"Kuan Hee, I am calling to tell you the military regime is facing a backlash from the police soon. It seems the police top brass are indignant that their Commissioner has been held incommunicado for a long time. Tension between the police and the army is simmering. Now is a good time for you to act. Get Jordan to do work for you. Over."

"Does it mean the police will help us rid Singapore of the dictator? Over."

"Yes. And it's going to be messy with the police and the army at loggerheads. Over."

"What shall I do with Jordan? Over."

"Get him to release the Police Commissioner. Over."

"How about the army generals? Over."

"He won't be able to release them. The moment he gives the order, his men will smell a rat. That won't be good for us. Over."

"Mr Walmsley, I'll try my best. Mr Walmsley, tell my Mum and Dad I miss them. Over."

"Thank you, Kuan Hee. And don't worry, I'll send your regards to your parents. Over."

"You guys heard what the Brigadier said. We've got to get to Jordan," said Kuan Hee.

"There are too many of us," said Kuan Hee. "The G men will be suspicious."

"What do you suggest then?" said Navin.

"I think—let's do it this way. Lina and I will approach Jordan. You and Tim will be the backup. You two will create a ruckus outside so that we can have some time alone with Jordan."

"One question, Kuan Hee. How will you know when he is Jordan and when he is Colonel Tee?" asked Navin.

"Yeah, how?" echoed Lina.

"Eh. That one—I have no answer," said Kuan Hee, tapping his fingers on his lap. "We'll watch them till Jordan's side appears."

"That'll be forever," said Tim. "We can't wait forever."

Kuan Hee paused in thought. "OK. We'll do this—Lina and I will watch them," said Kuan Hee. "You two will not be involved at this stage. Wait till we have had a chance to talk to Jordan. Then we will get you into the picture. OK?"

"That's fine by me," said Navin.

"Me too," said Tim.

Kuan Hee and Lina were again on Holland Road. This time, they reprised their artist routine. Both pretended to take perspectives of the Tanglin Complex and its surroundings. Then they sat down to work, drawing their creation. In the meantime, little Busy was flitting up towards the Supreme Leader's office on the second level of Tanglin Complex. Soon the robot drone was hovering over the Supreme Leader's desk. He was reading something on his large screen. It was a news Website— Channel Singapore. There was no one in the room. This time, the ceiling lights were switched on, flooding the room with brightness it had not been accustomed to seeing in a long time. The window behind the Supreme Leader's desk showed a clear view of the lush garden behind.

"It's strange—not like before."

"I thought Colonel Tee liked dark places."

"I thought so, too. This is unlike the Colonel."

"There's only one explanation—Jordan is in charge of his own mind now. It means—we've got to act, and fast."

"What if we are wrong?"

"We have no choice. Time is against us. Besides, we are out here. He's in there. It's safe. Nothing ventured, nothing gained, they say."

"I'll try using the microphone to talk to him."

Kuan Hee manoeuvred little Busy towards Jordan. Now it was just above his ears.

"Not too loud, or else someone outside will hear us."

"Here goes nothing."

"Jordan, Jordan."

Jordan tilted his head. He had heard something. He turned to his side. There it was—little Busy was hovering in front of him. Jordan looked perplexed.

"Who's that?"

"Jordan, it's me—Kuan Hee."

"Kuan Hee? Where are you?"

"I'm outside. I'm speaking through the drone's speaker."

"Is that really you, Kuan Hee?"

"It's my voice, for goodness's sake. Can't you recognise it?"

"Alright. Alright."

"How have you been, Jordan?"

"Well, sometimes I know where I am and at times I seem to be asleep. I can't put my finger on it."

"Jordan. Do you know you are your father right now? Oh gosh. I said wrongly. I mean, do you know your father's in you—in your mind, with you?"

"I kinda guess so, Kuan Hee. I see my father's men bowing to me and asking me for instructions. And sometimes I just lose consciousness and I don't know a thing. Then I wake up—like right now, and see myself again."

Jordan, your father is using your body. He's dead but his mind's alive and kicking. It's living in your brain with you."

"I thought so, too Kuan Hee. You must want something from me, Kuan Hee. What is it?"

Kuan Hee knew Jordan was smart. He was not only smart. His mind was quick too. He always got to be top student in polytechnic. And in university, he topped the examinations again. Maybe, that was why he was chosen as Student Leader at Temasek University.

"Jordan, I need your help. The Police Commissioner has been detained for ages on trumped-up charges. He is innocent. The police force needs him. Can you release him?"

"The Police Commissioner? Why did my father jail him? He's a good man. He's incorruptible. I remember during our polytechnic days we invited him to speak at a forum on law and order. He was humble but intensely knowledgable."

"Yes, I remember."

"I think you already know—your father has thrown into jail all who oppose his rule. The Police Commissioner is different from your father."

"Let me think—how to go about doing it. You know, these few days—I've been slipping in and out of consciousness. In my conscious times, I've been reading up, keeping myself abreast of happenings," said Jordan. "I read—you tried to kill me. Why? Kuan Hee? We are good friends."

"Jordan. Eh. I—it was a difficult decision for me," said Kuan Hee. "You were Colonel Tee—your father. At that time, I didn't know you could be yourself again. Honest. I didn't know. Otherwise—"

"But we are good friends—buddies, Kuan Hee," said Jordan. "How—aargh, my head, it hurts…"

"Men," called Colonel Tee. A minder came into the room. "I seem to hear some voices in the room."

"Sir, there's no one in the room."

"Are you saying I'm lying?"

"No, sir. Not that. I'll check the room again, sir."

"Why is my room so bright? Who switched on the lights? And who drew back the curtains?"

It was time for little Busy to fly back to the pair.

"Lina, we've got to get the hell out of here—the G men are turning the corner on the main road."

"They are making their rounds again? So fast?"

"Quick! Lina!"

CHAPTER 29

It was splashed on the front page of the local newspapers.

Army releases Police Commissioner

"Eh. Kuan Hee. Good news!" said Tim. "Here, take a look at the headlines."

Kuan Hee and Lina huddled over the newspaper.

"He's really done it," said Kuan Hee. "It's been a week. I thought he didn't want to help us. After all I tried to kill him."

"Could be—Jordan didn't get a chance to occupy his own mind. Maybe, the last few days, Colonel Tee was in control of Jordan's mind," said Tim.

"Yes, that could be it," said Kuan Hee.

"Good job, Kuan Hee," said Tim.

"Calling Kuan Hee. This is James Walmsley. Over."

It was the Brigadier again on the walkie-talkie.

"Mr Walmsley, I'm here. Over."

"Kuan Hee. Marvellous work. Simply marvellous. You have helped a great cause. Over."

"It's not only me, Mr Walmsley. It's also Lina, Navin

and Tim. They all chipped in. Over."

"Well done, all of you. My friends in the police force say they are preparing for a confrontation with the army. Now that the Police Commissioner is back safely, they see no reason to let the military destroy the country. Are you listening, Kuan Hee? Over."

"Yes, Mr Walmsley. I'm all ears."

"Sorry I'm being long-winded, boy. It's old age, you know. You just want to ramble on and on. Now, back to important things—listen carefully, my boy. The police are planning a pre-emptive strike on the Supreme Leader in two days' time. That's Friday. Do you copy? Over."

"Yes. I copy you. Pre-emptive strike on Friday, right? Over."

"Correct, Kuan Hee. The police commandoes plan to take over the Ministry of Defence and attack the Supreme Leader's office in Tanglin. ETA 5:00 a.m. Friday. Do you copy? Over."

"I copy, Mr Walmsley. Over."

"Now, what I need you to do is—get Jordan to release the army generals. Over."

"But, Mr Walmsley. The Colonel's men may not obey Jordan's orders. Over."

"That's where you come in, Kuan Hee. Your father has proposed something. Your father wants you to use AleXanders' rockets and laser systems to create a diversion at Tanglin Complex. Make it appear as if some people are attacking the premises. His minders will be kept busy. Then, get Jordan to run off with you. Are you following me so far, Kuan Hee? Over."

"Yes. Mr Walmsley. Where do I take him to? Over."

"Yes. I'm coming to that now. You go with Jordan to Dieppe Barracks in Yishun. Get him to personally escort the generals out of jail. You can do it, Kuan Hee. Over."

"It may be difficult, Mr Walmsley. If the soldiers see him alone, they may think something is wrong. Over."

"Not to worry, Kuan Hee. That part—the police will

help. The police will arrange for cars and men to go with you and Jordan. Over."

"I understand, Mr Walmsley. You want me to enter Jordan's office and get him to follow me to Dieppe Barracks to release the detained generals. Am I right? Over."

"Yes, that is correct, Kuan Hee. Do it on Thursday evening—before the police raids on the army. Over."

"I'll, Mr Walmsley. Over."

"And Kuan Hee, one last thing. Be careful. Colonel Tee is a treacherous chap and he was an army commando. He can kill you in the wink of an eye. Over."

"I'll be extra careful this time, Mr Walmsley. Over."

"Guys, you heard the Brigadier. Tomorrow's the day. We've got to get Jordan to come with us tomorrow evening."

"What's the plan?" asked Tim.

Kuan Hee, Lina and Tim pored over a map of Tanglin Complex. As he was describing their plan of action, Kuan Hee drew lines and 'X' marks on the map.

"Do we need the weapons?" said Tim.

"Nope, Tim. Not this time," said Kuan Hee. "I'll be using AleXander. Their arsenal will be enough."

"I don't think Navin can come. His father's funeral won't be over till late in the day," said Tim.

"Let him mourn his father first—it's more important," said Kuan Hee. "We'll make do."

"What time are we taking action?" said Lina.

"We will hop over around noon and we'll wait for an opportunity. We don't know for sure when Jordan will wake. We'll just have to watch them the whole day—from noon till the next morning," said Kuan Hee. "Tim, you take charge of Alex, and I'll handle Xander."

"OK," said Tim. "What's his phone number? I'll need to practise with him."

The sky over Tanglin Complex was threatening to open up on Thursday afternoon. Dark clouds were gathering over the horizon. Kuan Hee, Lina and Tim pretended to be survey assistants, clicking on number counters in their hands. They were huddled on the grass verge next to the busy road junction. Alex was sitting in Tim's backpack and Xander was lying in Kuan Hee's backpack.

"Remember to open the front panel on Alex," said Kuan Hee.

"I won't forget," said Tim.

The trio took turns to monitor the Colonel's activities in the office. They were sure the Colonel was in charge of Jordan's body, for the room was dimly lit and the curtains were drawn. They had to wait for Jordan to reappear. There just was no other way. The minutes dragged by, then the hours. It was still dark in the office.

"It's going to pour soon. The dark clouds are looming overhead now."

"We've got to work fast. There's no shelter from the elements for us here."

"Pray hard, pray hard that Jordan will awaken," said Lina.

"It's the only thing we can do," lamented Tim.

"Is that lightning I see up there?" asked Lina.

"Yes. I'm afraid so. Here comes the thunder," said Kuan Hee. The skies were rumbling.

"Kuan Hee. Look! On the screen. The room is bright!" said Lina.

"You sure are right, Lina. We must thank our lucky stars tonight," said Kuan Hee.

"But, there aren't any stars tonight," said Lina.

Kuan Hee flashed her a glare. "Joking, just joking," said Lina.

"Let's get going, guys," said Tim.

The men let Alex and Xander out of the backpacks. The two robots clambered up the slope towards the building. They adopted a prone position on the edge of the slope, ready to spring into action.

"I'll be with the robots; pass me your phone too. I'll take care of Xander too," said Tim. There had been a change of plan. Tim would control the two robots and the pair would go into the Supreme Leader's office.

Tim crawled up the slope and the pair separated from him. They took another path up to the building.

Just then, a figure came up behind Tim. It was Navin. He had come.

"Navin, you are just in time. I thought you won't finish with the funeral till very late," said Tim.

"My father would have wanted me to come here tonight," said Navin. "I'm sure he won't mind."

Here—take this phone. You control Xander with this phone and I'll control Alex with mine," said Tim. "Don't worry, I'll guide you."

"Kuan Hee, call Jordan. Tell him we're on the way," said Lina.

"Jordan, we're coming in. Please draw your bodyguards away," said Kuan Hee into little Busy's remote.

The pair climbed up a low wall into a long corridor. There was no one around. The cameras were pointing the other way. It was safe for them to move into the Supreme Leader's office.

The door to the office opened. Jordan was standing at the doorway.

"Come, quick," Jordan beckoned to them.

In the room, the pair were quick to strike a conversation with Jordan. They didn't know when his father would suddenly decide to pop in; they couldn't take any risks.

"Why are you here again?" asked Jordan. "It's dangerous here."

"We need your help again, Jordan. The army generals—we need you to release them," said Kuan Hee.

"But, I already told you it would be difficult. These men won't obey my orders. My father has told them if he gives them strange instructions, they need not act on them immediately," said Jordan.

"We have a solution, Jordan," said Kuan Hee. "Your men here won't listen to you, but the men in Dieppe Barracks will—your father hasn't got to them yet."

Jordan stood in deep thought for a moment.

"Alright. But, how do we get there? We are alone; the men in Dieppe Barracks will be suspicious," said Jordan.

"The police will help us. They will dress up as your bodyguards. They have got cars too," said Kuan Hee.

"I see, OK, alright," said Jordan. "Let's do it."

Just then a bolt of lightning struck the building, and its walls and pillars reverberated.

"Argh! My head—my head, it's painf—"

"What are you two doing in my office?" Colonel Tee boomed.

"Men!" he shouted.

But, his men had not heard him, for just then, a loud blast rocked the building. It was not thunder this time. It was Xander's rocket, blasting a wall of the building. Then there was another explosion. This time, Xander had fired his rocket at some plainclothes who were charging at him.

A third rocket from Xander hit an armored personnel carrier which had roared into the compound.

In the room, Colonel Tee retrieved a thirty-centimetre-long knife from a drawer in his desk, drew it from its scabbard and approached Kuan Hee and Lina. Lina was shocked stiff. Kuan Hee pushed her behind him. They backed away from the Colonel. But there wasn't much space left for them to retreat—the wall was only a metre behind them.

"You are the cause of this rift between my son and me," said Colonel Tee. "You shall pay dearly for this."

Colonel Tee was now lunging at Kuan Hee with the knife.

"No! No! Jordan! No! Jordan! He's your friend. He's not your enemy," screamed Lina.

Suddenly, Jordan woke. Seeing his father using his hand to attack Kuan Hee with the knife, he was in despair. Everything seemed clear to him now. The revelation came pouring into his mind.

> And shall come forth; they that have done good, unto the resurrection of life; and they that have done evil, unto the resurrection of damnation.

He knew what he had to do now.

He turned the knife into his own chest—plunged it deep into his torso and carved a path up towards his heart.

"No! Jordan! No!"

Then father and son collapsed onto the floor.

It was all over. The Tee Dynasty was over and done with. Singapore was free of the dictator's grip finally.

As Kuan Hee, Lina, Navin and Tim retreated from Tanglin Complex with AleXander safely tucked into Kuan Hee's backpack, Lina pointed to the sky.

"Look! Up there! The dark clouds are clearing. The wind is blowing them away," she said.

CHAPTER 30

In the ensuing days, the army tanks and armored personnel carriers rolled back into the army camps. Soldiers returned to their barracks and were placed under house arrest. Their coup leaders were arrested and put in prison to await court martial. Political party leaders detained during the army crackdown were promptly released and new elections were slated to take place in the coming months.

The Police Commissioner took charge of returning law and order to the country. He also presided over the repeal of the laws that the Tee military regime had passed in its short time in power.

It was also time for Kuan Hee's parents to return to Singapore. Kuan Hee and Lina were at Seletar Airport to welcome them. A military transport plane had flown them in from a United States Air Base in Australia where Kuan Hee's father, Professor Wang, had been recuperating under the watchful eye of his mother.

"Mum, Dad!" shouted Kuan Hee as the Wang parents stepped into the arrival hall.

"Uncle, Auntie," screamed Lina in sheer delight.

The Wang family were reunited finally. And Singapore was free again.

It was thanks to these twenty-something Singaporeans that Singapore could breathe easily again—but, for how long?—this was anybody's guess. Hopefully, perhaps, at least as long as the pair lived.

The End

Some of the places mentioned in this book are real:

313 Orchard
Anderson's in NEX Shopping Mall
Bukit Timah Plaza
Cavenagh Bridge
CentrePoint Shopping Centre
City Hall
Coney Island
Dieppe Barracks
Elgin Bridge
Jalan Naung
Hougang Avenue Five
Hougang Mall
Kovan Heartland Mall
Lucky Plaza
MacDonald's House
Maju Camp
McDonald's in Hougang Mall & Kovan
MRT Stations
New Era shop in 313 Orchard
NEX Shopping Mall
Ngee Ann Polytechnic
Orchard Gateway
Paragon
Punggol Promenade Walk
SAFTI — Singapore Armed Forces Training Institute
Seletar Airport
Tanglin Complex
Tang Plaza
Tanglin Mall
ToastBox in Hougang Mall
Wisma Atria

Temasek University in Yio Chu Kang is a figment of the author's imagination.

SINGLISH TERMS USED IN THIS BOOK

Ah Kong: Hokkien for grandfather
aiyoh: expressing shock or astonishment
alamak: expressing regret, shock or astonishment
enche: Malay for Mister; a senior NCO in armed forces
hah: expressing disappointment
Hock Chew: a Chinese dialect
Hokkien: a Chinese dialect
hor: added to the end of a sentence for emphasis
huang ah ma: Chinese for Empress Dowager
kakis: Malay for buddies
kopi oh kosong: Malay for black coffee, no sugar added
kaypoh: a busybody
kiasi: afraid to die
lah: added to the end of a sentence for emphasis
leh: added to the end of a sentence for emphasis
long time no see: not met each other in a long time
NSmen: National Service men
ORD: operationally ready date (completed NS)
roti prata: pan-fried flat bread
three-tonner: a military truck (weighs three tonnes)
tong fang: consummation of marriage
wah: expressing shock
wah lau: expressing shock
wah seh: expressing shock

The author lives with his wife in an HDB flat in Hougang, an idyllic backwater in the North-East of Singapore. They have no children.

ABOUT THE AUTHOR

Raymond Han is a late baby boomer in Singapore. He has worked as a banker, an editor and a teacher. After he left the banking sector, he found a second career teaching English Language to upper and lower secondary students in Victoria School, Montfort Secondary School, Greendale Secondary School and Hougang Secondary School.

Raymond also taught English at 'O' Level and General Paper to students in a private school for several years. He has a Specialist Diploma in Psychology (Counselling Psychology).

Besides teaching, Raymond has written three books for young adults. The first, a short-story compilation entitled 'Spice of Life: Singapore Short Stories', traces the trials and tribulations of some ordinary youngsters living in different periods of time in Singapore's modern history, from the late sixties and early seventies, through to the eighties and nineties. The second, 'Essential Guide to O-level English Composition', aims to help students build a systematic approach to tackling essay writing for the GCE O-level English Language paper. It incorporates a step-by-step method to teach students to write better paragraphs and essays. And the third, 'Mystery of the Battlebox', his maiden novel, is about some teenagers falling into adventure and discovering hidden gold.

He has also written several short stories, two of which appear in Life Accents, an English Language textbook for upper secondary, in Singapore.